I0591026

ORCS IN LOVE

A SEASONAL SPICE COLLECTION

TAMING THE OFFICE ORC

MATED TO THE SAPPHIC ORC

KIDNAPPED BY THE ORC

L.A. MONTEIRO

CHAOS ELF PUBLISHING

CONTENT NOTES

These stories feature MF and FF open door sex scenes with non-human characters, and some gender bending.

———

These books are set in the Seasonal Spice world and feature characters from across the series. The series order is in the back of the book. Prologues have been include so these can also be read as standalones.

CONTENTS

Taming the Office Orc

Prologue   2

1. Farah   3

2. Ben   9

3. Farah   18

4. Ben   25

5. Farah   33

6. Ben   39

7. Farah   42

8. Ben   45

9. Farah   50

10. Ben   53

11. Farah   56

One Year Later   58

Mated to the sapphic orc

Prologue   62

1. Erica   63

2. Olivia   67

3. Erica   72

4. Olivia   80

5. Erica   85

6. Olivia   88

7. Erica   91

8. Olivia   95

9. Erica   98

10. Olivia   102

11. Erica   105

Three Months Later   108

Kidnapped by the Orc

1. Emily   112

2. Lachlan   120

3. Emily   130

4. Lachlan   136

5. Emily   139

6. Lachlan   143

7. Emily   149

Three Months Later   155

More by the Author   157

TAMING THE OFFICE ORC

A SWEET AND SPICY ROMANCE

L.A. MONTEIRO

CHAOS ELF PUBLISHING

PROLOGUE

This book is set in the world of the Seasonal Spice Series

Everyone knows orcs exist. Four years ago, 200 of them appeared through a portal in the middle of a busy city street, 199 of them male. Now they're stranded, and making their way as best as they can in this world. Unable to breed with human women, their race will be extinct in a generation.

Some believe there are part orc women in this world, descended from ancient travelers. These women are called mystics, and legends say an uncontrollable heat will grip them when in the presence of an orc man. The exchange of body fluids is the only thing that will satisfy the heat.

But nobody believes mystics really exist, just like nobody believes in witches.

CHAPTER ONE

FARAH

I've always been different. In my coven I was the girl who couldn't do magic. In the city I was a freak from an insulated community nobody had ever heard of, and the secret of witchcraft kept me isolated.

I'd only been in the city for a month when my boss, Erica, took me under her wing. She said I was a natural with computers, and she could train me. She didn't ask too much about the coven - it didn't seem to matter. Erica believed in facing towards the future. After six months of working with her, I started to believe in my own future. I felt like I could belong.

It's a pity the coven wants me back.

"Call me if you're ever back in the city, Farah," Erica says next to me. We're standing in front of the elevator, waiting.

I nod, glancing at her. She looks tired tonight, dark circles standing out under her freckled skin, loose red hair shining under the fluorescent lighting. It should clash with the hot pink corporate dress she's wearing, but it doesn't. It looks just right paired with her black jacket and six-inch heels. She's only in her 30s, but everything about her screams 'boss.'

Her phone is glued to her hand as usual, but right now her attention is all on me.

I'm wearing a black corporate dress and a hot pink jacket, mirroring her look. I'm not embarrassed to want to be like Erica - she's my role model, but I'm still a bit of a mess.

Thick black glasses hide half my face, and I have trouble looking people in the eye. A mass of brown curls spring around my face, poorly restrained by a clip. In the coven, I would let it hang loose, hiding half my face. It's weird to think of going back.

My gaze tracks the row of lights above the elevator as they climb up. My handbag is slung over my arm and I'm holding a box of my things. Two birthday cards, a chipped coffee mug, a potted plant, and a pamphlet for a computer course Erica insisted I take. The coven will never let me study, but I appreciate the gesture.

The elevator finally chimes and the doors slide open. Inside is an orc in a boiler suit and a baseball cap. His green mouth curls up in a half-smile around small tusks, and there's a twinkle of mischief in his golden eyes.

"Ah Ben, the elevator's moving slowly. Could you look into that?" Erica asks him. She's not scared of him. He's been the maintenance guy for a month now. The company was hesitant about hiring an orc, but now he's considered a great addition to the office.

Ben nods in acknowledgement of the request. "Get right on it." Then his eyes slide to me.

I've avoided coming face to face with him since he started. My coven forbids interaction with orcs. I guess I can't avoid it now.

Erica gives me a kiss on the cheek and I shoot her one last sad smile as I step in.

When the doors close, it's just me and the orc.

"Hello, witch. Leaving the building?"

"Yes," I say, watching the elevator numbers descend, and trying not to look at him.

It's not easy. There are mirrors on either side of the elevator, and multiple orcs stretch in both directions around me.

His hair is in a long ponytail, strands hanging loosely around his face where they've come free from the baseball cap. The muscles in his long limbs speak of hard labor, but he's lean and tall rather than bulky.

He catches me looking in the mirror and grins at me.

My stomach flips. He might be green, but he's undeniably handsome. My body feels alert in a way it hasn't been for months. I haven't had sex since I left the coven, and when Rashid left me.

For a long time I was getting over the only relationship I knew, and then I was busy adjusting to my new life. A life without magic, which didn't involve orcs.

"I've been trying to get a hold of you, but you haven't responded to the notes I've left on your desk," he continues. He has a cheery patter and a thick accent. And his cheeky smile never seems to leave his lips.

I'm uncomfortably aware of how close we are in the small space.

No wonder the accounts girls talk about him so much. It's practically obscene, the things they say. Not that any of them would do anything. Everyone knows orcs are too big to... go there. A flood of images flash across my mind, bringing a flush to my face.

My jacket feels too hot suddenly. I'll have to take it off before tonight, anyway. Rashid would hate it. He'd hate all my new clothes, and unfortunately he's the one from the coven meeting me tonight. The thought of him is as irritating as sand in my shoe. It's way better than the despair I used to have, but it sits badly with my newfound physical discomfort.

The numbers tick down slowly. Four floors to go.

"Didn't know witches were on the diversity hire list," Ben tries again.

My irritation finds a new target. "Stop saying that," I say in exasperation, turning to him. "Someone will hear you. Witches are still hidden. We still remember the witch burnings." I don't ask how he knows I'm a witch. I've heard other witches talk about a sixth sense they have that can tell when another magical being is around. It's another talent I don't have.

"I know witches prefer to stay hidden in this world," he nods. "But I thought it would be nice for you to have someone who knows what you are."

"It's not," I say. My skin feels hot and prickly. Returning to the coven is reminding me of their strict rules, top of the list being to never talk to an orc. "If you were working here when I started, I would have gone somewhere else."

"I figure magic users should help each other," Ben says, and steps closer. The prickles increase, along with a wave of heat. He smells like musk, and weirdly, like vanilla. My mouth waters and I forget to respond. "I haven't met one of your kind this side of the portal. I could do with a few potions. Even if you're not trading your wares, you could put me in touch with a friend."

He's... everywhere. Filling the room, filling my senses. My gaze drops to the collar of his shirt, to the nape of his neck. The skin there is soft, ready to bite...

I take a deep breath and look away from him, back to the elevator lights. Two more floors until ground level. I need to get out of this elevator.

In the mirror, I see him reach out a hand to touch me. My entire body tenses, and I hold my breath. Panic fills me. I don't know what will happen if he touches me, but I know I'm not ready for it.

I turn around and face him, backing away before he can reach me. "Leave me alone! I can't help you. I'm leaving tonight. Find another witch to harass."

We're both blinking at my outburst when the elevator grinds to a halt.

Chapter Two

BEN

The witch swears creatively and drops her cardboard box and handbag on the ground. She sure is wound up. The motion throws her glasses askew before she fixes them. Something in the box cracks.

I'm not all that happy about it myself, but I know this lift breaks down regularly.

She's in one of those knee-length corporate dresses that are tight around her hips and float low around her cleavage. I'm surrounded by office workers every day, and I've never noticed that those outfits are as hot as fuck.

It's conservative, but it sits differently on her. It somehow emphasizes the wildness I sense in her, waiting to spring free.

Her face is flushed, and she peels off her pink jacket, revealing an expanse of brown skin on her arms. My cock responds like she's dancing naked on a pole.

I take a deep breath. It doesn't help. She's sweating, and it smells like flowers. Exotic ones, like the ones from my homeland. The scent presses against the hard wall of my control.

My heart is beating fast. An elevated heart-rate is a red flag, but we're still a day away from the full moon, so I'm going to pass it up to pedestrian level horniness.

In my homeland, I've seen orcs lose complete control when they're attracted to a woman. Our mating habits can be violent, and that doesn't translate well to inter-species romance. But I'm not like other orcs. I'm cursed. Letting myself lose control won't work for either of us.

I press a red button on the control panel of the left, then take a step back and sit down, leaning casually against a mirrored wall - as far away as I can get. My legs almost reach the full width of the elevator.

She throws her jacket and the clip from her dark hair into the box. "Are we stuck in here? I'm meeting someone from my coven to go back there tonight. I can't be late."

I wink and point to the red button. "There's an automated alert service. They'll be here within the hour." This isn't the first breakdown. If the service company were less reliable, the elevator might have been replaced by now.

Her lips are pressed together tightly, but she nods. "Ok, good. If I don't show, they're going to think I've run away, but I can make it within an hour."

She paces, wafting her scent around the tiny space. With her hair floating around her face like it is, that sense of wildness comes through again. It's in the way she moves. Gracefully. Almost cat-like. I could watch her pace all night.

I've never been this close to her before, and I honestly didn't realize my attraction to her ran this deeply. We've only seen each other in passing - down a hallway, getting into an elevator. No more than that. Enough for me to know she's a witch from the way my toes tingle. I wouldn't even notice the sensation if I didn't know it well from my homeworld.

After a few more moments of pacing, she slumps on the floor opposite me and drags her box to her, playing with the pieces of the pot she broke. Her face is squeezed into a frown, and she keeps rubbing her forehead with one hand.

It's easier to think when she's still. I unclench a fist, stretching the hand out to release some tension. Then I try not to breathe. We'll be out in an hour, and then I'll have a cold shower and a session at the boxing gym. I've been in worse spots.

I desperately need a distraction, and I've always been good at talking. "I'm Ben, by the way. We haven't properly met."

"I'm Farah," she says, shooting me a small smile.

"So you're going back to your coven. That sounds nice."

Her smile fades, and she takes a while to respond, like she's struggling to find an answer. "They're... traditional. Like they don't really understand technology."

"So, why do you work in a tech office?" I ask.

She looks at me before her eyes slide away. Before she opens her mouth, I know she's not telling the whole truth. "I'm here for research. The coven realized they need technology to stay hidden, but they still don't have a taste for it. And I don't have a talent for magic." She says it simply, but I understand enough about witches to know how much they value their powers.

Even if I didn't know witches, I know people. It's how I've learned to navigate my curse. Being a good listener has earned me a lot of friends, and I can tell she wants to talk. I can also tell she's an outsider, like me.

She looks at me apologetically. "I'm sorry I ignored you, but it's against coven rules to fraternize with orcs. And even if we could talk, I couldn't have helped you," she says. "I can't do magic myself, and my coven is insular - they're based in the country, well away from the cities. I had never spoken to anyone outside it before I got here. And they don't like orcs."

I ignore the comment about not liking orcs. I'm used to navigating around it. "Have you got any family meeting you tonight?"

"My ex-boyfriend." She doesn't look excited about it. "We broke up before I left." She pauses, as if debating how much to say, and I wait. My patience pays off as she goes on. "His mum didn't like me much. That might be why I was chosen to leave the coven in the first place. But I don't mind, now that I've been here. It was nice to see how the rest of the world works."

I nod, processing. Witches are big believers in strong bloodlines, and magic is hereditary. Without magic, this beautiful witch wouldn't be considered a good match. My fingers curl into fists at the thought of someone rejecting her over something so trivial. I want to hold her, make her feel desired, and wipe thoughts of this other man out of her mind.

But he's not my rival. She's not my girl. I don't get that option.

Instead, I say, "You sound like you enjoy the city."

A shy smile steals over her face. "It's nice. I'm good with computers. It's nice to be good at something." A waft of her scent overwhelms me when she smiles, and a shudder quakes deep in my belly.

I roll my shoulders and stretch out my stiff neck. Just another hour. It's not the full moon yet. And besides, I get to talk to her. I like talking to her.

"I like it in the city too," I say. "I like the offices. They feel right. They even smell right - under all the cleaning products, they smell stale, like a deep cave."

She's quirking her own smile at me now. "You don't see many orcs in offices."

"Doesn't fit the grunting and fighting stereotype?" I raise an eyebrow.

"No, I... I mean..." Her eyes widen and she blushes as she stammers. She stops and smiles when she sees I'm grinning at her. "I guess not all orcs are the same."

I like making her smile. And blush. And is she holding my gaze for a bit longer than necessary?

She looks away, her blush rising again. "Is it getting hot in here?" She picks up a pamphlet from her things and fans herself with it.

I grin harder. I've done a lot of flirting in my life, and I can tell when a woman's hot for me. Even though I'm technically biologically incompatible with most other species - there's still a lot of fun to be had.

I doubt she'll be up for anything like that, but at least I can enjoy the hour I have left. I just need to distract myself long enough to ignore my body's howling, primal demands.

"It is getting warm. Anyway, you're not all wrong about the orc stereotype. I still like a good fight to burn off steam." I watch her size up my physique through hooded eyes.

"A guy at my boxing gym got me a maintenance gig, and now I service a bunch of buildings in the city. Went independent a few weeks ago." I'm proud of it, and I'm happy she looks impressed.

"Another orc friend?" she asks. She's interested, but distracted, still fanning herself. She's quite red now - she puts a hand to her forehead as if testing her temperature.

"Human," I reply. "I've always gotten along with other species." I don't explain why. She doesn't need to know about my curse.

"I couldn't imagine living without my coven," she says.

"But isn't that what you've been doing? You've been here living and working for a while, yeah? That's pretty independent."

She smiles at me. "I suppose you're right."

My phone dings, and I check it. My stomach does flip-flops as I break the news out loud. "They've been delayed. It'll be another three hours." Not good.

She scrambles to her feet, face stricken. Sweat beads on her forehead. "They'll think I've abandoned the coven!"

Her pacing starts again, stirring the air. Her scent is all over me. There's nowhere to hide in this small room. I squeeze my butt, digging my nails into my fists, breathing deeply, willing my cock to soften. Any time apart from the full moon, I've been confident I have full control. This witch is proving me wrong.

"Pacing isn't going to help," I say tightly from the floor.

"What do you think will help, then?" she says, stepping towards me. "Is there any other way out of here?"

She's far too close, her gaze fixed on me. My heart picks up a notch. I stand suddenly, and I know she sees the lust written all over my face. Her chest is heaving, and her mouth opens as if to say something.

The urge to grab her and pin her against the wall is irresistible. Instead, I push her to one side, step towards the closed elevator doors and pry them open with my fingers.

They're stubborn at first. She stands closer to me, and the heat from her skin warms my back. If this doesn't work, I won't be able to resist whatever this is between us, and I don't know what that will mean. The thought gives me the strength to pull harder. It gives way with a groan.

Outside, we're stuck between floors, but the doors stay open on their own. There's enough space to climb down and jump to the lower floor. "Last resort," I say, and gesture for her to get out.

Chapter Three

FARAH

The cool air hits me as I walk through the night, away from the elevator. High-rise buildings and wide, well-lit streets make the walk to my nearby apartment easy most days.

Today my limbs are sluggish, like I've been lifting something heavy. I must be coming down with something. I don't feel weak, but I'm sweating profusely, and I'm running a fever.

I stop at a street corner to throw the cardboard box into a bin and sling my jacket over my arm. I'll have no use for anything in that box in the coven.

I stand for a moment, looking at the box, and pick the computer course pamphlet out, putting it back into my handbag. Maybe the coven will allow it. At least I can try.

I'm only a block from my apartment. It's a few more steps straight ahead. My feet don't seem to want to move.

To my right is a street I've never been down. It's dark in places, but it leads to a harbor on the edge of the city rimmed with expensive cafes. From here, I can make out lights twinkling in the distance.

I turn right. It's still early, and I could have my last dinner in the city at a fancy restaurant.

As I walk, my thoughts wander.

I almost threw myself on Ben in the elevator. Maybe I'm delirious because of whatever sickness is causing my fever. But he's nothing like I thought he'd be. Orcs are supposed to be scary, but Ben isn't scary. I talked to him as if I'd known him for years. I feel drawn to him. Maybe I always have, from the first moment I saw him, and that's part of why I've been avoiding him.

And I think he feels it too. There was a moment there when I thought he was going to kiss me. My whole body feels tingly at the thought of it. If I were bold, like Erica, I would have kissed him first. What would the coven think of that?

Remembering the coven sobers me. Rashid will meet me at my apartment, and I'll return to the world I knew. But when I lived there last, I was Rashid's girlfriend. Rashid comes from a great family and has a talent for potions. By his side, I was accepted. It was worth keeping the bruises from his occasional rages quiet.

Without him, I don't have much. I never knew my father, and my mother died a few years ago. I'll probably work in the town hall office with the only internet connection in town, organizing any technology for the coven. That's why they sent me here, after all. I can be useful, if not respected.

But this is selfish thinking. I was raised to think of the good of the coven. To think of the good for the community. The coven is family, and culture, and history.

Besides, where would I go otherwise? My thoughts drift to Erica and the pamphlet in my handbag. In my lifetime, only a couple of people I know have left the coven, and I've heard dark rumors the coven council won't allow it. But there's no proof, of course.

I'm so lost in thought, I don't notice the street is dark around me until two shapes split off from the shadows to my left and block my path. I stop abruptly, thoughts scattering with the hammer of fear in my chest.

They're orcs. Huge orcs. I appreciate how different Ben is from these monsters. They're hulking, almost fat with bulky muscle, creating a wall in front of me. Their faces are wide, their noses flat, and they smell of unwashed bodies. Thick tusks jut up from the sides of their mouths, and their eyes are glittering black pits.

There are scars visible on their legs and arms under their ragged clothing. One of them has a missing pinkie finger, the other a broken tusk. The one with the missing finger sniffs the air and speaks in a low drawl. "You smell good for a witch."

"You must excuse my friend," the one with the missing tusk says. His voice is softer, but his gaze is intent on me, which is no less frightening. "He's been starved of the touch of a woman for some time. It's usually a simple matter, but your scent is..." he breathes deeply and smiles. "Quite intoxicating. Perhaps we could get to know you a bit better. There's no need to be afraid."

My feet are frozen in place. I should run - back to the brighter streets. But they're close enough to grab me easily. I could scream, but I'm not sure anyone would hear. I'm trapped.

My muscles tense, readying to run. I've never felt adrenaline like this before - never been in this much danger.

My breath comes in sharp bursts, sweat prickling under my armpits. My heart pounds. I'm helpless. They think I'm weak and have no control. Just like the coven thinks I'm weak.

The one with the missing tusk steps closer. My fear turns all at once into a surprising, desperate, white-hot rage, and I let out a guttural cry and lunge at him.

A four-handed fist at my throat cuts my assault short. I'm lifted off the ground, and my feet kick helplessly. I choke, glasses askew. "Put her down! We want her conscious at first," the one with the missing tusk scolds.

The fear my rage had pushed away comes back in a flood as my feet land hard on the ground and the hand leaves my throat. I collapse in a heap, coughing and sucking in gasps of air. From the ground, I hear more than see the first sounds of fighting. The punch is a wet thud followed by a primal, loud roar no human could utter.

I look up as the orc with the broken tusk staggers back, facing off along with his friend, against Ben.

I wince as the orc with the missing finger punches Ben in the face. He staggers back and the baseball cap falls back off his head, letting his long hair loose down his back.

But then he turns back to his two adversaries, and his expression changes. He lets out a roar that shocks me, and he rips at his own clothing, shredding the cloth easily in claws that were blunt earlier that night. His powerful, hairless chest is bare and heaving, his boilersuit ripped to the waist. The sight of him ignites a flame of raw desire in my core. When he looks back at his adversaries, there's a thin layer of foam around his mouth, and his tusks have grown long and sharp.

He's still lean, but now I recognize it as an animal sleekness. He's a hunter, and the larger orcs are his prey. They see it too. Missing Tusk is already running when Missing Finger swears and stumbles back after him.

Ben chases them down the street, and they disappear out of sight while I get to my feet. I wince when I put weight on my right ankle. It's twisted. I can't believe I tried to fight those orcs! I'll be lucky if I can walk back to my apartment. Where Rashid is waiting to take me home. Right now, that feels like a good thing.

I get a few quick steps, leaning on the wall of nearby buildings, when Ben returns, stepping out of nowhere right in front of me.

It's still dark, and my breath catches at the sight of him. His bare, powerful chest is heaving from his exertions, his red eyes glowing like embers. The light from a distant streetlamp silhouettes him, and his claws still look sharp. His shredded suit is still there, but sitting so low on his hips it threatens to slide off.

He growls, low in the back of his throat, and goosebumps rise on the back of my neck. This isn't the orc I shared an elevator with today.

But he fought the orcs for me. "Ben?" I ask.

He steps closer, and I gasp. His eyes are red, yes, but his pupils are huge - dilated, like he's on a powerful drug. And they're fixed entirely on me.

The smell of his sweat permeates off him - sweet, wild and musky. My core tightens in response, even as the adrenaline from earlier kicks up again, sending my heart racing.

He's terrifying. He's intoxicating. I'm entirely not ready when he bends down, picks me up, and carries me into the night.

CHAPTER FOUR

BEN

When I get Farah home, I throw her onto the clean white sheets of my bed, heedless of her kicks and howls. I retreat from her quickly. The run through the streets cleared my mind from the haze of red I'd been seeing since the orcs attacked her, but my hands are still shaking.

Stepping away from her scent, I shake my head and take deep breaths. We're technically inside, but the space is large, so her scent has room to roam. The plants will mute it as well.

She stops kicking and stares around, mouth open. She looks cute like this, all disheveled, one shoe missing from the journey. Her face is flushed red, her eyes bright with fever. "Where are we?" she asks.

"My place," I say. The edges of my mouth tug up. I have enough of my senses now to be proud of what I've made.

It's a greenhouse on the top floor of a high-rise building, modified into an apartment. There is an actual apartment on the roof with a small room, kitchen and bathroom designed for a caretaker like me. But I like sleeping among the plants, under the stars. I've carved out space amongst the plants for a king-sized bed, a lamp, and a side table cluttered with books. A sturdy cable runs from the lamp back into the apartment outside.

When she's done gaping, she looks back at me. "Oh, so you talk now," she says tartly. She doesn't seem afraid, and her eyes linger on my bare chest and glaze over. She kicks off her only shoe as if she's not thinking and rubs at one ankle. She seems satisfied with it and finishes by stroking a hand over the soft white sheets.

When she's gone, I might never wash them again. It will be safe enough to masturbate to the thought and scent of her after she's gone.

And she will have to go. She's in more danger with me than she was with those thugs tonight. I know them, of course. They're the kind of orc that gives us all a bad name. They know me too, so I'm glad I've kept the location of my home a secret.

I shake my head, trying to think clearly. "We're safe from other orcs up here, so we can talk. I don't suppose your parents sat you down and had the birds and the bees chat about how you're descended from orcs?"

Her eyes open wide, and she lifts her hand and inspects it. "I didn't know my father. But he wasn't green. And neither am I."

My pulse is still too fast, my skin too hot at being this close to her. I back away a few steps, trying to walk casually. "Doesn't matter," I say. "You've heard of mystics? They look human but go into heat around other orcs. The symptoms are fever, sweating, and arousal."

She blanches and takes a deep breath. For a second, I'm captivated by the sight of her chest rising. My skin crawls with the urge to go to her. "That's why I was attacked?"

She's calm, and she knows what a mystic is. She didn't know she was one. That's all I need to know. "Come with me," I say. I slow down so she can follow, and notice she tests her weight on one ankle, but seems satisfied to put her entire weight on it.

I walk out of the greenhouse and open the door to the apartment, only a few steps away. The rest of the roof is covered in aggressively climbing vines and hanging plants, coating a lattice structure to make a loose roof. Pot plants and low lights dot the ground underneath them. It's a cross between civilized and wild - like me. Like her. The moon above is almost full, and the city lights twinkle around us.

"This is beautiful," she says reverently as we walk through. The traffic from below is muted up here. It's why I built it, although it's only used at Christmas and Easter for events by the corporation that owns the building. It's my sanctuary, and I want to tell her so. But I need to get her inside more than I need to talk.

I show her into the small one-bedroom apartment. Dirty baking dishes clutter the kitchen, and there's a pull-up bar in the living room, a couch, more books, and a laptop open on the coffee table. The bathroom is visible through the first door on the left. The bedroom is the second door. I take her in there.

There's nothing in the room but a four-poster bed and an empty window. The lights of the city twinkle through the window. It has a rough, solid metal frame, and it's bolted to the floor. There are thick chains attached to each of the bedposts with thicker padlocks. On one wall hangs a key on a string.

The reality of the shitty situation fate dealt me has never been more clear to me. I keep my eyes fixed on the bed as I explain. "I can't..." I falter but push through.

"Have you heard of a berserker? That's what I am. Great in battle, useless anywhere else. Violence can make me lose control, and sex between our kind can get heated. So I never trusted myself to mate with an orcish woman in my homeworld. Your scent is testing my control. You need to lock me up." I grab the key and hand it to her, looking at her for the first time.

Her gaze is fixed on the bed, and she hugs her own arms. "What happened to those orcs who attacked me?" She asks quietly.

"They're alive," I say, grimly, and press the key towards her. They're only alive because I didn't lose control completely tonight once I was out of her sight. Tomorrow night, at the full moon, will be a different story.

She takes the key, and I kick off my shoes, and get on the bed, lying spreadeagled on my back. "No more questions until I'm restrained."

She approaches the first cuff, swinging it open and closed. When the first padlock clicks into place, I relax.

"I'll be fine in the morning. The nights are more of an issue. I only turn in this world on the night of the full moon. I sedate myself, then as the drugs kick in, I lock myself in and throw the key away from me. An orc friend comes to let me out in the morning."

"Witches in my world used to give me a potion that prevented the monthly change."

"It's only on the full moon? That's tomorrow, right?" she asks.

"I usually change on the full moon without fail, but I can change any time. I spend my life managing it. Exercise helps me control it, and being around a low level of violence is like exposure therapy. But too much violence can set it off. And it's best if I avoid my own kind." Her eyes soften as she looks at me. I avoid her gaze. I don't want her pity.

"What about my heat?" she asks quietly, as she moves to one ankle.

"Well…" My eyes dart away from her again. "It will last a week or two at most, once every three months, but it's controllable if you're not around other orcs. You can stay here this time, and if you choose to ignore your orcish nature, your coven will be a safe place to escape it." My stomach churns at the thought of her so far away, but I know it's her choice.

"Does it hurt?" she asks.

"The heat is harmless, apart from some discomfort. While it's not safe for us to have sex, exchanging bodily fluids with a male orc will help ease your heat. You can have mine. We can figure the rest out later."

Her hand stills on my second ankle. Her gaze slides over my body and lingers on my cock, which is straining against my pants.

One of my ankles is still free. "I meant in a drink, or a pie. Something to disguise the taste," I say through gritted teeth.

She blinks and shakes her head, blushing. "Of course," she says, with reddening cheeks, and fastens the last shackle. "Is that comfortable?" she asks. I pull against them. They hold fast and I nod.

"The coven will think I abandoned them if I don't meet Rashid tonight," she says with a frown. "They have one phone and one email address which were both checked by me. I doubt anyone's touched them since I left."

"You can't go back down there," I say firmly, realizing that I couldn't stop her if she decided to now. "Your scent is like a beacon to orcs. Give it at least a couple of days."

She nods, frowning. Her hand on my ankle kneads my flesh, and I'm not sure she's aware of it. Her gaze drifts to my erection again. It twitches under her attention, and a red haze threatens the edge of my vision. I fight for control, but I know I'm losing.

"I'll prepare something for you in the morning to ease the heat," I say. "Sorry, but I didn't feel safe doing it tonight."

"But it's safe now, right? You're all tied up." Her voice is light and teasing, but her gaze is intent.

I should say no. But my tusks elongate and my back arches on the bed, and I can only growl as desperate hunger overtakes me.

Chapter Five

FARAH

I've never done anything like this before. But then, I've never been in this situation before, have I? I could be a half-orc. Or a mystic. Whatever. Words are irrelevant right now. And anything seems possible. The boldness that usually escapes me feels easily at hand now. I'm high on lust, and the knowledge of Ben's lust for me in return.

The fever in my blood sings at the sight of him tied up on the bed. The size of his erection straining under his pants is hard to look away from. But the rest of him deserves some attention too. The only man I've been with is Rashid, and he never made me feel this way.

Ben's naked chest is chiseled and taut with his exertions as he twists on the bed. His boilersuit shifts low on his hips.

I reach out and slide a hand across his abdominals. He stills as I touch him, his pupils huge in reaction to my presence. His skin is so hot it's almost burning.

He growls low, almost a purr. The sound causes a strange zinging between my legs, and my temperature spikes. I undo one of his buttons, and it's enough to reveal a smattering of black curls and the straining shaft of his erection. I undo another and it springs free.

I knew orcs were big. Knowing and seeing are two different things.

My skin feels tight and sensitive as I stare at him, and clothes are far too restricting. I step back and he huffs a breath of air in objection, irritation coloring his face. It clears when I reach for the zip at the back of my dress.

When it slides down my body, his gaze tracks across my bare skin. I've never felt more completely at the center of someone's world. I unclip my bra, letting it fall to the floor. My nipples pebble in the cool air.

He throws his head back and roars, the sound so loud it feels like a physical force. It rattles the window in its frame. I take a step back as he pulls sharp claws and strong limbs against his restraints, desperate to get to me.

Fear cuts through me, and a burning starts deep in my lower belly. Moisture soaks my underwear, and I'm sure he can smell it. My breath comes short and quick, and I'm not sure if it's fear or desire.

I shake my head at the confusion. If I didn't believe him before that I'm part orc, I believe him now. Any human would have run from him.

His black and red eyes track my movements as I walk to the foot of the bed, away from his swiping claws. They're full of lust, but they're so wild... If he gets free, he could tear me apart. He might not be able to stop himself.

But I could die right now, in need of him. The fever that grips me feels like it's going to burst out of me. Ben promised it would be better with a taste of him.

I tentatively touch one of his ankles again. He thrashes harder, snarling and straining. The bed shifts underneath him, but it's bolted to the floor. I pause, but the restraints hold. He can't reach me. I crawl my way up his calves, and then his thighs, mounting the bed until I'm kneeling between his spread legs.

There's pre-cum pooling at the tip of his erection. I touch it with the tip of my finger and put the fluid back into my mouth, tasting him. I'm gratified by the smolder in his eyes and the stilling of his body.

Having such a powerful creature at my mercy is intoxicating. And arousing.

"Would you like me to touch myself, Ben?" I ask, stroking fingers across my sensitive nipples. I barely recognize my voice, teasing and seductive. But I'm enjoying toying with the monster. He hisses and leans forward against his restraints. His tusks are more like fangs now, and they look sharp. "I'll take that as a yes," I say, and dip a hand to my sodden sex.

He holds his breath, watching me, but as soon as my fingers meet my clitoris, I know I can't wait.

I bend down to take him in my mouth, bracing a hand on one of his powerful thighs, my other hand relieving myself. Every muscle in his body tenses and he hisses, eyes closed tight as I suckle at the tip of his cock.

He grunts and groans, hips shifting underneath me restlessly. I take him deeper into my mouth.

He explodes, and I swallow in surprise, choking at the overflow. I haven't yet found relief.

When I sit up, wiping at my mouth, I notice a fading blue tinge to my hand.

Ben stares at the ceiling, blinking. His eyes are golden again, his fangs small, his claws short.

"Ben? Are you okay?" I ask.

"Holy fuck, yes. Just give me a second. I'm seeing stars."

"Okay," I say, and can't keep the grin from my face.

It doesn't take long for him to speak again. "Thank you. That was incredible. I was going to say no, but you just proved it's possible."

"And you seem okay now, right? Do you still need to be chained up?"

"I'm not sure, but it's probably safer. And you can sleep in my bed in the greenhouse."

"Oh." My face falls. Of course, that's what this is. I knew that. It must be awful for him to lose control of himself, and my presence causes it. The pit of my stomach shouldn't be dropping with rejection, but it is.

"Okay, I'll go," I say, covering my breasts. I'm glad I'm still wearing underwear.

"Hey, no - wait," he says, trying to sit up, bound hands out beseechingly at me. "I definitely did not mean to say anything to get you to cover up. I would prefer it if you never wore a top ever again. It just might be safer..."

That, and the genuine distress in his eyes, stops me. But my hands are still covering my breasts. "Ben, you said you'd never been with an orcish woman. Does that mean you've never..."

The twinkle is back in his eyes as he grins at me. "I discovered the joys of inter-species sex and got very good at satisfying women in other ways. I was plenty satisfied by what we just did."

Beneath my hands, my nipples harden. Ben may have had release tonight, but I have not.

Something in my face must show it, because he says, "How are you feeling? Would you like to see what else is possible?" He glances down at his soft penis. "I'm calm enough for the moment. And I'll have to stay tied up, but we can get creative." The cheeky grin he shoots me zips straight to my core.

CHAPTER SIX

BEN

I've spent my entire life avoiding my people, in particular orcish women, in this world and in my homeworld. Friends and lovers are easy to find in other species. Family is not. But I'm a danger to everyone around me, and I can't offer a future to anyone like that.

But as I look at Farah straddling my waist, completely naked, blushing, it's hard to keep that reality in the frame. She's beautiful. A dream. Something I never thought possible.

Her fever has gone down, which means our fluid exchange so far has worked, but the lust hasn't left her eyes. Good. An orcish heat is uncontrollable, and I want to know she's choosing this of her own volition.

When she leans down to kiss me, a cloud of her floral scent comes with her, and I let out a sigh. Her lips are soft, just a press. I've never been more aware of my heart beating. It's fast, but not dangerously fast. This woman is a drug, and I'm glad I'm restrained. My cock is already stirring at the slow kisses she's giving me, but I still feel in control.

My tongue darts out and licks at her lips and she gasps. I take advantage of her open mouth, kissing her more deeply, entwining our tongues until she makes a soft whimper of need. I huff a chuckle, and she pulls back, batting my chest and smiling at being mocked. "What? I can't enjoy giving you pleasure?" I ask.

"That might be hard with your hands tied," she says in between kisses.

"But my mouth is still free," I say with a grin. It hides my nervousness. I want to pleasure her, but I know how large my fangs get when I turn. There's some risk involved in this. But the idea of tasting her... She pulls back, eyes wide. "Only if you're comfortable," I say, grin fading.

She smiles shyly at me this time, and her thighs squeeze around me. "To ease my heat, we both need to exchange fluids, right?" She asks.

I nod, my smile returning. "It's practically science."

After a few more kisses and a bit of maneuvering, she's straddling my shoulders and lowering her sex to my mouth. She leans forward toward the headboard to keep from collapsing back.

My cock comes back to life as I lap at her juices. She tastes delicious. Primal. Like something I never knew I always needed.

I strain against my bounds, needing more, lifting my head to get higher, sucking and nibbling on her clitoris until her legs are shaking and she's collapsing, nearly suffocating me. I'm not complaining.

Before long, she cries out and floods my mouth with hot liquid. I drink it down. Every moment feels right. She lifts off me quickly, and she looks shaky as she climbs back down me again.

Her head collapses to my chest before she lifts it to smile at me. Her skin is tinged green, and her limbs seem sleeker somehow – thicker with muscle. Otherwise, she's unchanged, and the color fades as I watch. It's true then. She's orcish. She kisses me gently, slow and seductive, and I smile through it. This is a woman satisfied, and I was the cause. And I've kept control.

When she puts her head back to my chest, I'm not ready for my time with her to be over. She's a miracle - I know that much. She would be a miracle for any orc in this world, but she's especially a miracle to me.

Chapter Seven

FARAH

If my presence makes it harder for Ben to keep control, I should stay away from him tonight. I feel safe with him tied up, but I can tell he doesn't like it when his berserker grips him.

But his body is warm and I'm still buzzing from the best orgasm I've ever had, and I'm not ready for it to be over yet.

I keep my head on his chest when I ask, "So you've... never done that with an orcish woman before?"

"No. Never thought I would, either, what with there being no orcish women in this realm, apart from Olivia. And it's not like she doesn't get enough harassment." Everyone knows the name of the only female known orc in this world. He says her name warmly, and I can tell they're friends.

"The friend who ties you up every month..."

"Yeah, that's her. Pretty much my only orcish friend. Neither of us really fit in with other orcs. I feel sorry for the other males, though, sometimes, that the only woman to come through is a lesbian." He huffs a laugh, and the twang of jealousy in my chest eases. "But I don't know the men, really, except in passing. They either revere me for the way I can turn the tide of battle or hate me for choosing to lock myself up."

"Are you lonely?" I ask.

Something flashes across his face. A sadness that's there and gone in a flicker. "Only among my own kind. I learned long ago how to make friends with others." I think of his amiable smile, and the way I opened up to him so quickly. "Did you have a lot of friends in the coven?" he asks.

"I had Rashid... but no, no real friends."

"That's not so surprising, when you're different," he says, but I barely hear him.

The reality of my future life in the coven hits me. I won't be going back to anything that's mine, and my life will be mapped out for me, controlled for the collective good. In the past, I thought there were no other options. But now I've been in the city, and I've seen how other women live their lives. And tonight, I've had a taste of who I could be if I'm not at the coven. I'm not ready to give that up.

"I don't think I want to go back."

There's a long pause, while my stomach sinks at the implied rejection.

His voice is soft and grave when he speaks. "I found out I was berserker when I was a teenager. When my first girlfriend and I were having sex for the first time. We didn't get very far." He sighs deeply. "I would love you to stay here, but I would always be worried about what would happen if you did. I won't let that happen to you." He says it like a promise. "Besides, you won't need me. You'll have your choice of 198 suitors who will be very excited to meet you."

I don't want anyone else. And given the strain in his voice, I don't think he does either. "Tell me about mystics," I say, to distract from the sting of his rejection. "The coven only had snippets of knowledge."

"Well, you're half orc, but that's only the start. You could have visions, and your fluids could have healing powers."

"Healing powers?" For the first time, I raise my head and look at his face. "Could they help you?"

Chapter Eight

BEN

I frown down at her question, and the excitement in her eyes. A frisson of hope runs through my chest, but I push it down. I've had false hopes before, and it's painful when the reality of my condition comes crashing back in.

I do feel calm with her in my arms. I thought it was the rosy afterglow of our time together, but my cock is hard again, with her naked body pressed against me.

She looks down and squeezes my shaft, making me gasp. "After you drank my juices earlier, you could be cured of your berserker. But we can't tell when you're calm. So I'll have to excite you again."

My blood roars in my ears. But I clench my buttocks, fighting her. If I turn now, she could get hurt.

"I can't believe this thing could really fit in me," she teases. *Sweet Jesus, this woman is going to kill me.*

"You really are a witch," I say. "But you need to get away from where I could bite or claw you." She presses a soft kiss on my lips, completely ignoring me.

When my eyes open, I find her looking at me in question. "Would you want me to stay if we settled your berserker?"

"More than anything in the world," I say passionately.

"And I would be your first orc lover," she says. There's a possessiveness in her gaze, but her eyes are clear. "And I want to find out if you'll fit." She's milking me now, pumping her fist up and down.

With her hand on my cock and the taste of her still on my lips, I can barely squeeze out a protest through a clenched jaw. "Get out of range of my claws,"

She obediently sits up, throws a leg over me, and lowers her crotch to mine.

When her hot sex hovers over my cock, I start to pant. My eyes roll back in my head, and my hips thrust at her in tiny jerks, willing her to mount me. But strangely, I feel myself. I look at my hands - my claws aren't out.

My gaze turns back to her. She's holding herself in place with her hands and knees, bracing herself over me, waiting. She waits until she holds my gaze. "Ready?" she asks.

Her face is flushed, but she's in control. I nod. She lowers herself on top of my cock. She doesn't put me inside her, but instead slides her slickness around my thick member. It's a delicious torture, feeling her stretch around me.

My eyes drift down to her pert breasts, to her folds wrapped around my cock. Then back up to her face - her eyes are heavy with pleasure, but she's still her.

This isn't like before, when she sucked me and I lost all sense of reason. She's not a slave to her heat or soothing the beast. This is Farah and me. The hope I felt before surges anew, and this time I let it.

When she lifts herself up and presses herself down around my cock, I savor every gasp and wriggle. Every time she moves she slips me further into her. It doesn't take long for us to confirm she's a mystic, if there was any doubt. No other woman I've been with has gotten this far.

She's only halfway on me, and her small body looks tiny skewered on my giant member. It's a deliciously filthy erotic image, now sealed into my memory forever.

Her eyelids flutter, her mouth falling open with pleasure, her head falling back.

"Are you okay?" I ask.

"Yes, " she says. A radiant smile lights up her face as she looks at me. A chord of something painful strikes in my chest - more than desire. More like need. I need this woman. "It feels incredible."

She begins her slow ride again but her movements are soon jerky and her gasps pained. Just because she's a mystic doesn't mean it won't be a tight fit. "Kiss me," I say. "I'm still in control. And there's no rush."

She leans forward and kisses me, my cock still inside her. "Farah," I say, wanting to keep her in this moment forever. "You know you're beautiful, right? When I wake up tomorrow, I'm going to think I dreamed all this. You're my dream-girl."

She smiles. "I bet you say that to all the girls riding your cock." The dirty words make red stir at the edges of my vision, and my heart leaps in anxiety, and she senses it and sits up, watching me calmly.

I keep her gaze. She's not watching me with fear, or even with compassion. She's watching me like I'm hers. It gives me the strength to push the red haze away. When she rides me again, pressing herself up and down until my shaft is slick with her, I'm fully in control. Even when I'm fully wrapped in her glorious pussy.

The red flush in her cheeks turns completely green, and her limbs elongate and thicken with muscle. She closes her eyes, and when she opens them, they're red and predatory. Her orcish nature has fully claimed her, but she smiles at me, and I can see she's still herself, with some extra new qualities. She wraps a hand around my throat in ownership and squeezes, partly cutting off the bloodflow to my brain, but leaving my breathing free.

It's a traditional claiming, part of orcish culture, and I don't know if she knows about it or is acting on instinct. My body doesn't care. Her hold is enough to make my hips press up into her, desperate for the pleasures only she can bring. But the loss of control gripping me is mating lust, not rage. I'm gratified by her groans of pleasure.

I buck for her until she squeezes around me and cries out in pleasure. The fresh wave of hot liquid around my cock brings on my own release. A universe of stars explodes across my vision, and all my muscles clench, then melt into liquid relaxation.

When she lays her head on my chest, I mean to stay awake, to savor the awe of her, but sleep drags me under.

Chapter Nine

FARAH

Over lunch, I'm smug. We're at Ben's place, on the couch, and Ben hands me a plate with a tuna toastie on it. He's shirtless, wearing low slung blue jeans. The smell of baking fills the small space. "I guess the experiment worked, huh?"

We've been having sex for most of the morning, which has cleared my heat and given further proof that my fluids are controlling Ben's berserker.

I've been green for longer, and Ben says I get stronger when I shift, which at the moment is only during sex. I like it. It feels powerful, like I could take on the world. Or maybe it's Ben that's making me feel this way.

He frowns. "Tonight's the full moon, which is the real test. But I think..." he takes the plate out of my hands and puts it on the coffee table, then takes my hands in his. "I think I should still invite Olivia over in case I turn. She can help control me if I do turn and help you if you're injured."

Although I know it shouldn't sting, it does. My whole life is pivoting towards Ben. I wish he believed in us as much as I do.

But when he looks up, his brow is creased with worry. "I don't want to hurt you."

"You won't," I say. "I think we might be destined to be together. I believe that, and soon you will too."

"I barely even believe you're real, dream girl," he says with a smile and a kiss. Then he stretches. I watch appreciatively. "But I should really go to the boxing gym. I've got a routine on full moon days, and the exercise helps soothe the berserker. If your heat plays up, you know what to do." He nods to the apple pies cooling on the kitchen counter. One of them contains his semen.

"I'd like to go back to see Erica. To ask for my job back," she says.

"I offer you a garden paradise, full of leisure and apple pies, and you want to go back to work?" His mischievous, sexy smile flips my stomach.

"But first I need to swing by my apartment," I say. He frowns. I talk fast to justify it. "It's daytime. I can take the apple pie with me, and I'll go straight there. Nowhere near the wharf where the homeless orcs congregate."

"Back by dark," he says sternly.

"I'll be back far before then," I say. And I mean it.

It's 6pm when I rush towards my apartment door.

I should have known that Erica would hire me back on the spot, and immediately put me to work on a project so riveting I lost track of time. The day was a blur, with my heat only at a tolerable burn. It's nowhere near as intense as I was fearing, but then Ben and I have done a pretty good job of controlling it.

I want tonight to be special, and that means grabbing the lingerie I was too self-conscious to change in the bathroom at work. Fortunately, Ben's rooftop is only a block or two from my apartment. Plenty of time.

I smile to myself when I turn the key in the lock. Ben's going to love it.

My smile fades when I see who's inside.

CHAPTER TEN

BEN

The sunset sky is streaked with brilliant orange. It looks magnificent in my garden. Any other day, I would stand here and appreciate it. But Farah's not back yet, and the sun is slipping low.

I was calm until sunset really started. Ants crawl under my skin at the anticipation of the full moon. *Where is she?*

Pacing isn't helping, and I'm running out of daylight. Without her here, I will change, and I'll need the chains in the bedroom. But she could have been attacked or hurt out there.

Anxiety sickens my stomach and decides for me. I leave a note for Olivia or Farah, in case I miss them, and head out into the city.

Her office is empty, but her scent is everywhere. She can't be far.

When I reach her apartment, my heart is pounding. It's the change.

I followed her scent trail the entire way here, right up to the third floor. When I smell her through the door, I let out a sigh of relief. We can still make it back to mine in time if we leave now.

Then I hear her cry out and smell blood. Her blood.

The door splinters easily under my fists. Farah is in a black work dress, holding one bright red cheek, and blood trickles from her mouth. There's a man facing her, who's now turning towards me.

Then his throat is in my fist, his feet dangling from the ground. I walk him to the balcony and shove him through the glass, stepping us both out. His head lolls to one side, his eyes closed. He touched what's mine, tried to take her away from him, and he will die. Another step and he'll go over the edge.

"Wait!" she cries out behind me. I turn my head to her, breathing her in. The delicious one. Mine. "Don't kill him!" she says. "Ben, you don't have to do this. He tried to convince me to go back to the coven. But I won't go back. He can't hurt me now."

I turn back to my prey. I want him gone, then I will take her. But her hand is on my shoulder, distracting me, and when I turn my head, she presses her mouth to mine, between my fangs. I taste her blood where he hit her, and it ignites a fire of need in my belly.

I drop my prey and he collapses atop the broken glass with a crunching sound. I have new prey now.

But she's backing away from me now and says. "Come and get me." I roar at the challenge and race after her.

Chapter Eleven

FARAH

I've never run this fast. My muscles are stronger, vitalized with my orc blood. I think perhaps Ben could still catch me in this state if he wanted to, but he seems to enjoy the game.

He's not the only one. When he burst into the door tonight and took Rashid by the throat, even with his red eyes and ferocious claws, I knew with a certainty that he would never hurt me.

With him on my heels now, my blood thrills with anticipation, not with fear. My sex is dripping, and the heat is again fully upon me.

It's a long way to the top of Ben's building, and Ben chases me up the stairs the entire way.

By the top, even my orcish strength is failing me. My legs are jelly and my throat is on fire, but I'm still running when he catches me under the lattice of vines.

He tugs at an ankle and I throw my hands out to brace myself, but before I can land face-first, he's caught me in his powerful arms. He puts me down on my back, and I don't resist when he shreds the bottom half of my dress with his claws and rips my underwear from me.

When his mouth closes over my sex, my eyes roll back. The hardness of his elongated tusks press against me, while his tongue inelegantly laps at me, devouring me for his own pleasure rather than mine. He makes grunting animal noises, and his claws greedily clutch at my breasts.

It's obscene, and I love every second.

When his thick tongue pierces me, I cry out, my back arching as an orgasm takes me. I flood his mouth with juices.

I'm still gasping when he says my name.

"Ben?" I sit up on my elbows and look down at him. His fangs have gone down. His eyes are normal, although his face is blanched in shock. I smile at him, smug again. "I think we can call the experiment a success."

His face crumbles in tears and I sit up and squeeze him in a hug while he cries. He doesn't have to tell me it's relief. I let him get it all out, knowing that he's mine, and I'm his, and we'll never have to be alone again.

ONE YEAR LATER

FARAH

We're lying on the greenhouse bed naked when we find out the news. The sun is low on the horizon, and orange light streams through the glass. A gentle breeze stirs my hair. Ben's reading a book and I'm scrolling my phone. When I show him my screen, he swears and takes the phone from me.

"They've found another mystic," he says with a frown.

My heart leaps in my chest. I think about the life we've built together, in secret, on this rooftop. Not much has changed for us, except now Ben spends a little less time at the gym and a little more time with me.

I'm studying the computer course Erica recommended around work, and I've moved into Ben's rooftop apartment. Our life is pedestrian - human.

As for the witches, the coven hasn't tried to come after me after the night Ben knocked Rashid unconscious. And we've never told other orcs about my existence - even Olivia. Ben doesn't want to fight other orcs for me, and I don't want anyone else.

We knew our lifestyle couldn't last forever. My coven might come back for me, and the orcs can help protect us from that. We planned to tell the orcs eventually. But the months slipped by and neither of us wanted to break the bubble of happiness we'd built.

But now things are different. In more ways than one.

My hand creeps protectively to my belly. "This is a good thing," I say. "We can't hide forever. Not now." I smile, unable to keep the joy from my face.

His eyes widen. "I know nothing about orc pregnancies," I say.

He laughs out loud and puts my phone down, rolling so he's on top of me. My arms wrap around him easily,

"You really are my dream," he says, and kisses me.

"And you're my family," I say, tears pricking my eyes.

He kisses me gently, before we prove to each other in more than words that we belong together.

MATED TO THE SAPPHIC ORC

L.A. MONTEIRO

CHAOS ELF PUBLISHING

PROLOGUE

Everyone knows orcs exist. Five years ago 200 of them appeared through a portal in the middle of a busy city street. 199 of them were male. One was female and utterly disinterested in men.

Two months ago the first mystic was discovered – a part-orc woman who appeared human until an uncontrollable sexual heat gripped her when she met her first orc man.

There are likely more mystics hidden among the human population, giving hope to the orcs that there will be a future generation. But so far no other mystics have been found...

CHAPTER ONE

ERICA

There are officially no good men left in this city. And my date isn't going to show up.

I twirl the Chardonnay in my hands in the dim light of the bar. At least the wine is decent. And at least nobody is going to notice my misery.

The bar buzzes around me with the sound of chatter and clanking glasses. It's filling up fast, so I'll have to give up my four-seater booth soon. I wasn't thinking about sticking around, anyway. It smells like old beer and sweat and the seats are sticky.

Most of the other women in the room wear denim jackets and miniskirts, and they're about a decade younger than me. A couple of biker guys with tattoos lounge at the bar.

With my tight corporate yellow dress, heels and black jacket, I stand out. This isn't a bar I'd choose to be in normally. But it's close to work, and I'm unlikely to run into anyone I know.

I dial my best friend, since I have nobody else to call, and try not to dwell on how pathetic that is. It rings out. I fight the feeling that I'm destined to die alone. I finish my Chardonnay, putting my phone in my handbag with a sigh.

This was my second date with Ted, the accountant. Good family, good job, handsome and polite. He had potential.

I didn't sleep with him - a good choice. I made fun of how boring his career as an accountant must be - bad choice. Is it my problem that men are so sensitive? He could have at least declined the second date instead of standing me up.

I think back to the mild-mannered man in the glasses who met me in this bar last week. He looked scared of his own shadow. I should have expected he wouldn't have the guts to tell me he wasn't interested.

I pull my jacket on and flip my red hair over a shoulder, noticing a cute but young biker checking me out. I raise an eyebrow at him and he smiles, nods at me respectfully and looks away.

At least someone thinks I'm fuckable.

The thought of a one-night stand doesn't even cross my mind as I walk to the toilet.

I'm not up for a quick fuck. I'd much rather do a few more hours in the office than waste my time.

I'm only dating at all for the end goal. After years of focusing on my career, I've got it where I want it to be, and now it's time to focus on the rest of the package. Husband, kids - the works. The stuff my best friend Sally gave up her career years ago to have.

In the past few years, I've started envying my best friend Sally's domestically driven lifestyle instead of shuddering at it. The late nights in the office get lonely, and what's the point in making Senior Partner when there's nobody to share it with?

And what I want, I get. That's how it usually works, anyway. It's how I've gotten everything I have in life. Dating is proving to be an exception.

It's only when I'm leaving the toilet I notice Ben and Farah in the back, tucked into the darkest booth in the room. His arm is casually draped over her, his janitor's cap pulled low. With his baggy jacket on, most people wouldn't even notice he's an orc, and she's a human. They could only get away with it in a dive like this.

My surprise at seeing them gives way to concern. I don't have kids, but I have staff, and Farah is one of my most promising. And she's pregnant. Unless there's something I don't know about, that can't happen with Ben.

I frown, stopping my thoughts whirling before they get too far, and do what I do best - take action. I approach them.

It's only when I get closer, I notice the tall woman with the long dark braids sitting across from them. She's got her arm draped over the booth beside her, showing off lean muscle and smooth, dark skin.

My stomach tightens when I see her. She emanates power and confidence. Which I meet the way I always do - head on. I slide in beside her, and she turns to look at me.

CHAPTER TWO

OLIVIA

Five minutes earlier

"So, you're pregnant?!" I ask, my voice going up an octave. "No, wait, just a second." I drink the rest of my beer in one deep swallow. It's full, so it takes a couple of moments. When I slam it back down, I take a deep breath, and they're both still looking at me hopefully.

"Okay, you're pregnant." Much better. The beer has taken the edge off.

My brother Tom and I have spent the past two months testing half the women in the city to find another legendary mystic. And I expect he's been trying his best to get his fiancé knocked up. Meanwhile, my old friend Ben was starting the next generation of orcs in secret.

I laugh and shake my head. Ben raises an eyebrow at me.

"Sorry, I just thought of something. I love my brother, but I kind of love that he doesn't get to be first this time."

"We were hoping for some support?" Farah asks, smiling. I like her instantly. She's a beauty, with long dark hair and a sweet expression. I've never seen Ben this relaxed.

"Of course. Anything you need is at our disposal," I say, shaking my head. "I wish you'd come to me sooner. We've been expanding our facilities, and there's a place we could take you..."

They exchange a look. "We were hoping to stay in the city," Ben says. "As long as possible, if we can."

They hold hands, resting them on the table, and look at me hopefully. "We've both worked hard to build a life here. I like my job, and our home," Farah says.

"And I don't want to lose my freedoms," Ben says, with a pointed look.

Ben and I go way back. In our homeworld, I knew him as a berserker. As a lesbian in the royal family, I was about as outcast as he was, and equally trapped in my role.

We've both found freedom in this new world, although I still have a part to play in uniting our people. In this homeworld, nobody expects Ben to be a fighter. I understand why he doesn't want to give up his freedom.

I'm considering how we'll make it work when a redhead slides in next to me, right under my arm, and gives me a challenging look with some of the prettiest green eyes I've ever seen.

She's wearing a tight yellow knee-length dress that somehow looks right on her pale skin. And she smells amazing - like spicy wildflowers from home.

My mouth instantly waters, and I resist the urge to bury my hands in her hair. I'm not doing so well with ripping my eyes away from her, though. But fortunately, she's staring back at me just as hard. And she's sitting so close, I can feel the heat from her skin.

"Er, hi Erica," Farah says. Ben moves his arm away from her.

The redhead turns away from me, blinking as if coming back to herself. "Oh, hi! I um..." She swallows, then frowns, and shuffles away from me slightly. "I was wondering what you two are doing here, looking so cozy?" She folds her arms. "Care to explain?"

"And an introduction?" I drawl. I wasn't planning on picking up tonight, but plans can change.

Farah turns red. "Um, this is my colleague, Erica. I didn't think I'd see you here... I can explain..."

"She's a mystic. They're pregnant," I interrupt. Ben shoots me a look and I shrug. "You can't keep it a secret forever."

Erica looks back at me, and her eyes flash in challenge, but she turns back to Farah.

Farah shrugs, eyes wide. "That about sums it up."

I'll give it to Erica - she takes it pretty well. She stares at Farah, then Ben, and then me. When her gaze turns to me, I resist the urge to shuffle in my seat. I've faced down men three times her size with a less intimidating stare. And I've gotta say, it's pissing me off as much as it's turning me on. "And where do you fit into this?" she asks.

I lean in until she can smell my breath and say, "I'm Olivia. I must say, I'm loving this whole sexy school mistress vibe you've got going on."

She scowls at me, but I don't miss the way her pupils blow out and her breath catches. And that sweet floral scent - holy crap, it's filling my world right now and I'm not sorry.

Ben clears his throat. With difficulty, I rip my eyes away from Erica and look at him. He's frowning. "Um, Olivia... Erica's scent has changed."

I look back at the woman beside me, who's clearly collecting herself. I'd like to feel smug about that, but I'm finding myself equally frazzled.

"What does that mean?" Erica asks sharply.

"Oh my god, I can smell it!" Farah says excitedly, and leans forward and clasps Erica's hands, voice in a loud whisper. "I'm so glad you're a mystic too!"

Erica looks at her in horror.

Chapter Three

ERICA

It's too hot in here, and Olivia is sitting too close. Or not close enough. She was eye-fucking me earlier in a frank appraisal I've never had from a woman before. It made something stir in my lower belly. But now she's frowning, looking at me warily.

I know what a mystic is - a woman with orc blood, who can transform into an orc. Someone not human. Like Olivia.

I'm painfully aware of the inches between us as she shuffles further away from me and takes her arm out from the bench behind me. My stomach sinks a little. I don't want her to pull away from me.

I don't know what's come over me. I experimented in college and have never had this strong a reaction to a woman before. Or a man, for that matter.

But Olivia is obviously not interested.

"We need to get her out of here. She won't be safe until she chooses a mate," Ben says urgently.

I shake my head. "I'm not a mystic," I say. "That's absurd. And I'm not going anywhere but home," I say to Olivia.

Her face is serious as she shakes her head. "Wait," she says.

Her shoulders are tense. Maybe that's why I stay. That and the bizarre urge to reach out and touch the corded muscles in her shoulders. She's clutching her empty beer glass with both hands, looking at it more than she is at me. "I'm sorry. I know this is hard to understand, but I need you to come with me. Ben and I can both smell you're a mystic. Now your true nature is active. Before you find a mate, that scent is like a beacon to other orcs. I can protect you, take you to an isolated place so you can learn about your nature and choose a mate for yourself."

"A mate?" I ask, incredulously. The word is absurd, but it twinges some deep longing inside me. "I don't even know who you are."

"Olivia Johnson," she says, and quirks me a smile and raised eyebrows. She lifts a hand, which slowly transforms into a green claw. "Recognize me now?"

I gasp. I recognize her - the bodyguard of Tom Johnson. And judging from the last name, also his sister.

I also know enough about mystics to know they can activate around orcs. But I frown and look at Ben. "If I'm a mystic, why didn't I activate around Ben? We've been working together for months."

Olivia frowns and shakes her head. Her hand is back to normal again. "No idea. Maybe it's adaptation at play. Whatever the reason, mystics are our hope for the next generation of orcs." She says the last part with resignation and takes Ben's half-drunk beer from his hands and downs it before slamming it down on the table empty. "So, it would be my honor to help protect you until you select a mate." She nods grimly and pushes me out of the booth.

She's much bigger than me, so I have little choice but to stand. But I don't appreciate when she grabs my wrist and starts walking me out the door. "Hey, let me go!" I say.

As we walk past the bikers at the bar, the one who was eyeballing me earlier stands up. "Dykes aren't welcome here," he says to Olivia.

She rolls her eyes and ignores him, continuing to drag me out of the bar by one wrist. I scramble to stay standing on my heels.

He breaks a bottle of beer over her head. My breath catches, but she just pauses, sighs, and says, "I don't have time for this," and keeps walking. But I see a trickle of blood where the glass has cut into her forehead, and a sudden rage fills me.

I twist around in her grip and stomp a heel into the guy's foot. "Asshole," I say. Olivia is still holding my hand, and she pauses and looks at me for a moment before continuing to drag me outside.

She lets my hand go when we're out the door. The bouncer watches us, bemused.

"Hey!" I say. "You can't just drag me wherever you want. Even if I am a mystic, I still have free will."

I turn around and march off in the opposite direction, shimmying my tight yellow dress lower. It's not a dress designed to storm off in. She doesn't follow.

I head to the busy inner city, near my apartment building, and away from any orc-populated areas. The streets are thick with evening shoppers and people who've poured out of their day jobs commuting home. I'll be safe here until I can get home and decide what to do next.

About a block away, I realize my mistake. There's an orc lounging against the side of a building. The streets are busy enough, but after seeing Olivia take a bottle to the head from that biker, I know there isn't much that can slow an orc down.

He sniffs the air, spots me, and heads towards me. Apparently, whatever Ben and Olivia said about my smell is right.

My heart pounds in my chest as I turn around and head away from him fast. I walk into an air-conditioned department store, speeding through the racks of clothing to reach the escalators. I sneak a look behind me and see him following, his green skin pale under the fluorescent lighting. He has two orc friends. And they're looking right at me.

Oh shit. My breath comes in short bursts, and I stumble as I get off the escalator and sprawl on the floor near a perfume counter. They're going to catch me. Why do I wear such tight dresses to work?

A hand reaches out to help me up. It's Olivia. She's not smiling. She helps me up and puts a hand on my elbow, steering me away from the escalators. The line of her body is tense, her movements quick and efficient as she moves us.

An orc roars behind me. The entire department store turns to look. A woman screams and people cower away as the orcs race up the escalator to meet us.

I expect Olivia to run. Instead, she places me behind her with a sigh. I hold on to the back of her singlet. She smells spicy but clean, like cloves, with a salty overlay of sweat. It contrasts with the sanitized sweetness of the department store. It shouldn't smell good, but I resist the urge to press closer and breath her in.

Despite our situation, she doesn't seem scared. Her muscles are tight, like she's ready for anything.

"Not now, Jared," Olivia says to the orc. "You'll get your turn."

His eyes are red, his chest heaving against a shirt that's barely covering his muscles. He looks worked up. The orcs behind him are in similar states, grunting and huffing. Other shoppers are actively running away from the orcs.

"You cannot keep her from us, bitch," Jared says with a snarl.

She sighs again. "Seriously? I'm a bitch now? We played Nintendo, like last week." She shakes her head. "We won't keep her from you. But she's one of the first mystics we've found."

He roars. "I will fight you for her!"

"That's the hormones talking. If I leave her here, you'll rip each other to pieces trying to get to her. Tom and I have thought about this. This isn't the homeworld. We don't want to lose half the men in a mating frenzy. You will each have time to win her."

I look at Olivia in alarm. A mating frenzy sounds terrifying and violent, and none of the hulking brutes huffing at me look appealing.

One orc behind Jared runs forward. "Enough talking! She is ours!"

The third orc grabs the back of his shirt and holds him back. "She's mine!" he yells. Jared punches him in the nose.

They start to tussle and Olivia hurries me away to a lift. They're still fighting as the doors close. She runs a hand through her braids. "Sorry about that. They're not always like that, honestly. Mating can get animalistic."

I stare at her. In the small space, her scent is stronger, and I notice she's keeping her mouth open, not breathing through her nose. And she doesn't sound scared at all about the orcs after us. Her calm, protective confidence makes me feel safe. It's also incredibly sexy. The air in the lift feels like it goes up a few degrees.

I remember her closeness from the bar. Now I know who she is, I recognize her orc form from TV. The human version of her doesn't look much different. But I'd still love to see her green and muscular, maybe oiled.... I blink, clearing the vision. "You're not affected by the heat?" I ask.

She shrugs a shoulder, not answering me. The elevator doors open to the roof, and a helicopter is waiting.

"Ready?" she asks. She doesn't yank me forward this time, but now that I've seen the orcs fighting over me, I have a clearer idea of what I'm in for.

And I'd take Olivia's cool-headed, no nonsense approach any day. I take her hand.

Chapter Four

OLIVIA

I lean well away from Erica in the helicopter, away from her damn scent. It's not easy in the tiny helicopter, with only two seats in the back. The roar of the engine surrounds us, helping distract me. We both have headsets on, if we want to talk, but neither of us have used them.

I've smelled mystics before - I was there when my brother first met his fiancé, Summer. But Erica triggers something in me Summer never did. It was hard to let go of her hand when we got in the helicopter.

I look at Erica from the corner of my eye. She's texting someone. Now and then she glances over, lips pressed into a thin line like she's pissed off. At least she came with me.

She's a spitfire, this one. The only other mystics I've met are Summer and Farah, and they both have a sweetness that helps tame the orcs they're with. Nobody would call Erica sweet.

When she stomped on that biker's foot, it surprised me, but also it didn't - I've known her for about twenty minutes and every second has been like an arm wrestle. And why does that give me such a lady bar?

I email my second in charge, a human called Al, who manages Tom's security with me. Then I text my brother Tom.

> Found a mystic. Taking her to the island. Made a bit of a scene in a department store. Have briefed Al to cover it up, but the orcs will gossip. - Olivia.

> No time to lose. Have her ready tomorrow. - Tom

My brother never was one to mince words. But he's right - we're on a clock.

It makes no sense why I triggered her mystic side, but if she's anything like Summer and Farah, she's going to go into heat pretty soon. My turning orc might speed that process up, and if anything, I need to slow it down. She's not for me. I don't get to have a mystic - that would be selfish, when there are so few of them, and they're the only hope for the future of our race.

I swallow down the bitterness that comes with the thought.

I've got a good life, and a healthy sex life. Unlike the other orcs in this world, I don't have compatibility issues with human women. And there are plenty of women who like the idea of a big, strong orc woman in their bed. Never mind that none of them have gotten under my skin quite this much.

Summer rolls her eyes at what she calls my groupies. I rarely shift into human form when I pick up. I wonder how Erica will react when she sees me all hulked out.

The thought makes me suddenly aware of my breathing, and I slow it down. I can't go green on her. I'm here to help her pick the right mate.

I glance over at Erica again. She's pale and slim, with light freckles on her nose under her makeup. The skin on her neck is almost translucent, and I imagine pushing that red hair back and kissing her in the soft hollow there.

Her eyes are fierce when she catches me looking and shoots daggers at me. It's insanely sexy. And in a day or two, she'll be someone else's.

Fuck it, maybe I'm a sucker for punishment. "What's the problem?" I ask her. The microphone activates and I hear the open line in my ears when I speak.

"I can't be pissed off about this situation?" she asks, throwing her hands up.

I can't help it, I laugh. I don't know why. Maybe because she obviously doesn't care that the pilot in front of us can hear everything.

She doesn't look at me. "You know I was stood up tonight," she says. "And the only fucking reason I'm dating at all is because I think, you know, it's time. So, I'm wasting my time on these fucking losers, because I want a future that I choose. And now... that entire future is gone. So, I'm fucking pissed off about it, okay? I like to have choices in my life."

She looks at me then, with those pretty green eyes aflame with irritation, then looks away.

We sit unspeaking while the engine roars for a long moment. I consider that, and how I should respond.

Then I take her hand. She looks at my hand on hers, then back up at me.

"I'm a lesbian born into a traditional orcish royal family. My only role in my world was to make more orcs. My family wanted me to hide what I am, or lie about myself, but I wouldn't. I've had to fight, to have any choices at all.

You might be a mystic, but you still have choices," I say. "I'll make sure of it."

She looks away but keeps her hand in mine. And we stay that way until the helicopter starts to descend.

Chapter Five

ERICA

"This is fucking ridiculous," I say, "I'm not sick, I'm just... going through a process," I explain to the HR manager over the phone.

I'm standing in a cream-toned luxury apartment on a tiny island off the east coast of Australia. Through a large picture window, waves crash against rocks on the beach only a few meters away. The sound of seagulls cuts through the double glass.

When we descended last night the view from the helicopter was only dark shapes and blinking lights. In the morning I could appreciate the breathtaking view. The sea around us is clear blue, the sand fine and nearly white, and there's not a ship in sight. The Australian coast is a distant black line on the horizon.

Olivia's people have taken care of everything. After I arrived last night, I was equipped with a phone charger and a laptop, a spare black corporate dress, and this apartment all to myself.

Despite this, I am not at all relaxed.

"Look Erica, I'm sorry, but it's all over the news, and we have to be careful. Tom Johnson's people have advised us you'll need at least two weeks off for your hormones to settle. Even remote work isn't a good idea," she says down the line.

"And why can't my boss, Roger, tell me this himself?" I ask.

She's silent at that. Because my boss is a coward, that's why. And he'll have to explain to me where he's sending all my clients. To that sniveling asshole Cameron. I sneer into the phone and throw it at the glass.

A long crack shoots through the large pane. I freeze, but it doesn't break.

I sigh and fall back on the soft couch.

There's a knock on the door. What fresh hell is this?

I go and open it. Olivia has a knuckle raised to the door, the other leaning against the doorframe. She raises an eyebrow at my flustered energy and curves a smile at me.

She's wearing a thin singlet that clings to her slight and muscular frame, and cargo pants. And her gaze is fixed on mine in a way that makes my stomach fizz.

Just because I've never been with a woman before doesn't mean I haven't appreciated the sexiness of this one. I stalked her online and found I'm not the only one.

Olivia's had quite a few celebrity women on her arm in the past few months. After scrolling a few images of women in sparkly dresses pressed up against Olivia, my body got all hot and prickly and I slammed a fist into the laptop keyboard. Fortunately, those things are pretty hardy.

But apparently this means nothing. Only a male orc can help with my heat, which could lead to painful cramps if I don't pick a mate soon. Apparently it's like menstrual cramps on steroids.

Thinking of my impending fate, and Olivia's arms around supermodels on the red carpet, lends a razor to my words. "I know you're an orc now. It's okay if you're not human around me," I say. "You're never human around other people."

"It's safer this way," she says, straightening up. Her gaze slides away from me. "I came to tell you your first date is here. He'll be here in five minutes. Get ready." She turns and walks away down the hall, not waiting for my reaction.

Chapter Six

OLIVIA

I stand in the hallway outside Erica's room, listening at the door for trouble. And really hoping I hear nothing else, like the sounds of her mating one of the other orcs.

It hurts having to do this. But I picked the orcs who are the smartest, toughest, and most capable of handling Erica's shit. They're our most eligible bachelors.

A couple of human guards with stun-guns stand with me. They're well trained, and their hands sit warily on their triggers. I wonder if they ever thought they'd be chaperones for this weird orc dating service.

The other orcs don't ask about who she is. They couldn't give a shit, really. But I know they'll love her - every orc wants a challenging, fiery woman.

Meanwhile, she means everything to my people. There's exactly one eligible, compatible orc woman in this world, and she's it.

Alric went in first, two hours ago. He's considered to be handsome, and he can string a sentence together. When he slid on in he winked and popped a pec muscle at me. He was holding a bunch of flowers and wearing a tuxedo. Tom must have specially ordered him one that fit.

He lasted twenty minutes before storming out. "That bitch isn't worth it," he said, barreling past me down the hall, flowers still in hand.

Now Hans is inside. He's a more sensitive kind of guy, so I figure he might last longer.

They're in there for a few minutes when I hear the crash. The surrounding guards look wary, and I'm about to go in when the door swings open. Hans hurries out and shuts the door behind him. "Hopefully they aren't all like that," he says, and shakes his head. "I'm sorry, Olivia." Then he, too, heads off down the hall.

"Fuck," I say to nobody in particular, and bark at the guards to stay where they are while I go into her apartment.

There's a ceramic vase smashed on the floor near the door. I step over it, entering the open-plan kitchen and living room. She's pacing, agitated. Behind her, the glass has one large crack in it. I suppose I should be grateful it's holding together.

Maybe a big glass wall wasn't the best idea to cage the hormonal, raging mystic. The ocean crashes against the rocks outside in a foamy mass. The sky is gray, and it looks like a storm is coming.

"What is going on?" I ask.

"I'm not a fucking breeding mare!" she screams at me. I duck a ceramic ornament she throws at me. Her eyes are red. I'm pretty sure she's not aware of it.

Her chest is heaving. She's going to go into heat soon, and if she doesn't pick a mate, it will not be comfortable. She doesn't have time to meet all 197 eligible orcs.

"Okay," I put my hands out as if soothing a wild animal. "Maybe I went about this wrong. I was picking what orcs considered eligible. Maybe you need to tell me what you're looking for in a partner. Like maybe you could tell me about your last boyfriend?"

"There is no fucking last boyfriend," she explodes, glaring at me with rage. Then she flops on the couch and cries.

CHAPTER SEVEN

ERICA

Well, this is humiliating. I'm a hot, hormonal mess, crying on the couch in front of my lady crush.

Olivia freezes, shocked at the abrupt tonal change. She looks afraid to touch me. I'm not surprised. I was a total bitch to the orcs she sent in to court me, and I know she's only trying to help.

She finally comes to the couch and puts an arm around me stiffly as I pull myself together. "Hey. It's okay. I'm sorry, I shouldn't have assumed. If it makes you feel any better, I've never dated a dude either."

It does not make me feel better.

"It's not the same." I shake my head. "I just thought there would be time for a family later. And I've seen women do the stupidest shit for love." I scowl, and Olivia smiles at me.

It's nice having her this close. I thought there was something between us on the plane. I get the impression she doesn't open up to many people. As soon as we were off the plane and interacting with other orcs, she was a commander - and she didn't take my hand again.

"It's only recently that I've wanted more than a career." It's shocking to me, saying this out loud. The only person I've told I've been interested in a family and started dating is Sally. The only person who's known I'm terrible at it is Sally.

I look at Olivia. Her arm is still around me, and it's doing a weird combination of calming me down and winding me up. My whole body feels strung tight. Neither of the orcs who met me today felt like this.

I thought I wanted to date so I could have a baby, but maybe I also wanted someone to listen to, who'll hold my hand, and just by that simple touch make me feel... alive.

And sure, maybe I'm not red carpet material, but I'm not too shabby. And when she looks at me like she is right now, I think she might be interested too.

But I don't want to move too fast in case I spook her. "How about you? Ready to settle down with one of your celebrity girlfriends? Or not the settling kind?" My stomach flips a little when I remember the pictures of her with other women.

"Nah," she says, and I catch my breath as I notice her gaze flits to my mouth, my neck, and back to my eyes. "Never found the right girl."

I can't tear my gaze away from hers, so I see when she bites into her juicy bottom lip.

It's more than enough incentive for me to lean forward and kiss her, but she stands up before I have a chance. "I've got another guy in mind," she suggests. "Just one more. A different kind of orc. Don't worry - leave it to me."

"Of course," I say, my stomach sinking as she leaves the room. And then, I'm full of rage.

I grab my phone and dial the only person who can calm me down when I'm like this.

"What is it? Did you find one?" Sally asks, excitedly. She sounds like she's somewhere quiet. She's known where I am since last night and she's unreasonably upbeat about my situation.

"No," I say. "It's as bad as dating normal men, with a lower education standard."

"Ouch," she says. "But I hear brains aren't the assets that make orcs so appealing..."

"Well, that's disturbing."

"Oh my god, are you not an orc, and are you not in heat right now? How is the thought of orc cock not exciting to you?"

I sit on my couch with my head in my hands. "I have no idea. All I know is I'm angry for no reason, and apparently if I don't pick a mate soon, I'm going to be in pain with my heat coming on. But I'm not attracted to anyone but Olivia."

"Ooh," Sally says. Like most people in love, she's sickeningly wanted me to settle down for years.

"Are you not listening? Apparently, lesbianism isn't an option in the orc world. We're all biologically driven. According to the doctor who looked me over last night, my reaction to Olivia is purely biological and misguided. It has nothing to do with latent bisexuality."

"That sounds like a lot of hetero-normative bullshit to me," Sally says. "I've never heard of you being this interested in someone before. It sounds like you really like her."

I think back to Olivia protecting me in the department store and holding my hand in the helicopter. "Yeah, I think I do," I say, while my heart pounds in my chest.

CHAPTER EIGHT

OLIVIA

I'm standing in the hallway and I'm about to call an orc I think might be a good option for Erica, when my phone rings. It's Ben.

I walk away down the hall away from her door, leaving the security guys to it - most of the rooms are still empty, so it's just rows of closed doors, beige carpet and fluorescent lighting.

"How is she?" Ben asks.

"She's proving to be..." I struggle to find the right word. "Fussy," I land.

He laughs down the phone, which causes some tension to ease in my shoulders. "Yeah, that's Erica. Farah says she doesn't date much - or ever. And she's used to being in control. I was wondering how she was going to deal with the alpha bullshit most of the orcs dish out."

"What do you think she's looking for, then?" I ask.

"Well, I was thinking about that," he says. "And I've known Erica for a while. We've been physically close enough to ignite her mystic, Olivia. But it didn't trigger off until she met you. And the way you two were looking at each other..."

I shake my head. "You know that can't happen," I say softly.

"Found someone else then?" he asks. "Or just not interested?"

"No, Ben. You know why." If there's anyone who understands me, it's Ben. He was alone for years before he found Farah, even in our world. He was too afraid he'd go berserk and hurt someone.

He knows about my family, about my obligations, and my sense of duty to the orc people. He knows I couldn't take a mystic away from the male orcs when our people might die out in a generation.

"I know why you think you don't deserve happiness, Olivia. But I think maybe you should find out what Erica wants before deciding for both of you. If she doesn't want another mate, you might not be taking something away from anyone."

When he hangs up, I sigh and stay looking at the phone. I know Ben means well. And he's right - I haven't been interested in a girl like this in a long time. Erica has gotten right under my skin, cut through all my defenses.

But my people come first.

I pick up the phone again, and make the call for the third orc, a softer guy this time, who Erica might not devour before needing to mate.

Chapter Nine

ERICA

The orc Olivia sends in next is different. "Hello, I'm Cliff," he says, and extends a hand to me. He's smaller than the last orcs, with close-cropped hair, and lighter green skin. He has a friendly face, a quiet manner and intense eyes. I don't hate him.

I shake his hand, surprised. "I'm Erica. It's nice to meet you. Would you like a seat?"

He sits next to me on the couch, our legs propped up towards each other. It's the strangest set up for a first date ever - intimate, and yet, in this almost untouched room, clinical.

He's not throwing his weight around like the last two orcs who came in here or trying to dominate me. He smiles at me and cocks his head, considering.

My body feels... strange. I'm agitated, and I have constant butterflies in my belly. I drop his hand.

"How are you feeling? Olivia told me you're close to your heat. I hope you don't mind me saying you smell delicious." His red eyes smile at me, and there's heat in his gaze, but he's not openly ogling me like the last two orcs.

He has some control. Olivia chose well.

"Tell me about yourself, Erica," he says.

I blink. The last two orcs almost immediately started talking about sex, which irritated rather than aroused me. This feels more like a human date, which I should prefer. But it just reminds me of the man who stood me up in the bar, and the pressure that this could be my last chance to find a mate.

And when I find a mate, I could have children. A life like Sally's, although a bit more green. With an orc like...

My mind stalls, unable to picture a future with the orc in front of me. Instead, I think of Olivia, in orc form, sitting next to me on this couch, biting into her lip. My stomach flips, and I stand, my decision made in a rush.

I don't care about children, and apparently neither does my body. I know what I want.

"I'm so sorry, Cliff, but I think I've decided on my mate," I say firmly.

His eyes widen in surprise, but he's gracious when I show him to the door.

When I open it and he steps out, Olivia raises her eyebrows at me, and steps into the apartment after me.

When the door shuts behind her, and we're almost at the couch, I turn around, stand up on tiptoes, and lean in to kiss her.

She freezes for a moment that feels like an eternity.

Then she wraps her arms around me. Her tusks elongating mid-kiss. When I pull back to look at her again, she's all green. She's bursting against her tight tank top, her limbs elongated and muscular.

Taller than she was in her human form, but very similar looking. And that clean but spicy clove scent is stronger than ever.

She's the hottest thing I've ever seen. Wetness instantly spills between my legs. They forgot to get me new underwear, so there's nowhere for it to go but on my thighs.

Olivia's pupils dilate, and she sniffs the air. "Fuck," she says, and kisses me again, open-mouthed and hungry.

I try to climb her, but she rips at my dress, tearing a shoulder as she rips it from my body.

Meanwhile, I drag her tank top over her head. She's wearing a sports bra she helps me take off, leaving her glorious, full breasts at mouth level.

I squeeze and suck at them, hands hungrily exploring her body.

She moans and her red eyes flash when she throws me back on the couch and bends her head to my sex. I grip onto her head and hold on for dear life as her tongue lathes me.

I had sex with a couple of guys when I was young to see what it felt like. It felt nothing like this. She's a wild thing, hungrily devouring me, and when she presses a finger into me, I convulse uncontrollably and groan deeply.

I've never made a sound like that before in my life, and I'm shocked at myself when she lifts her head from my sex, smiles at me and wipes my juices from her mouth with the back of her hand.

Chapter Ten

OLIVIA

Okay, maybe that shouldn't have happened. But I can't keep the grin off my face when I look at Erica stretched beneath me. She's so fucking beautiful, and she tastes as good as she smells. This might do nothing to ease her heat, but fuck, it was satisfying feeling her lose control beneath me.

I wish Ben were right - I wish I could have her like this all the time. The attraction is there, all right. And she looks happy now, not uptight and wound up like she did before. I crawl up her body and kiss her deeply, reaching for her cheek with my hand. "Hey gorgeous," I say. "I hope that helped."

She huffs a laugh, but her eyes are intent when she trails a hand down my body and tugs at my belt. "Only partly," she says, and smiles at me.

Fuck, this woman is a demon.

At some point we have to talk about the future of my people, and that as much as it kills me, eventually she'll have to pick a mate she can breed with.

But right now, it's hard to think about anything. With her naked, the spicy scent of her all over my tongue, and her gaze fixed on my tits like she's seen nothing like them.

I sit on the couch next to her and pull down my pants. My underwear is already soaked. I only get my boots off when she puts a hand into my underwear. "The good thing about being with a woman," she says, with a hot breath on my ear, "Is that I already have some experience of what feels good to me," and she strokes a finger along my clit.

My eyes roll back into my head, and I don't resist when she lowers her mouth to suck at my nipple. She bites the sensitive flesh and I cry out and arch up off the couch.

I'm not usually one for pain in the bedroom, but it's a standard part of orcish mating, and Erica is part orc. Maybe that's why she bites me again, and I wrap a hand around her throat, pushing her back onto the couch and straddling her and claiming her mouth again.

Her hands peel down my underwear and she reaches around. When she touches my clit, it feels incredible. The orgasm swells from that sensitive place until it feels too much, almost overwhelming, like she's got a hold of me....

She pulls back, eyes wide. "Um, Olivia?" she asks. Her eyes are gorgeous - they're almost glowing now, a soft red against her green face.

Her features are the same, but her limbs are longer, stronger. In the past few moments, her orcish side burst out. And she's even more beautiful. My clit pulses where her fingers touch me.

I follow her gaze to where she's looking at our crotches. And see she's holding my cock.

Chapter Eleven

ERICA

Olivia jumps back from me, and her new cock wobbles. I stare. I mean, how could I not? But also, I couldn't look away if I tried. It looks like her clitoris has extended and swollen. It's... hot. My core aches to have her inside me.

"What the fuck?" she says, running a hand through her braids and looking completely freaked out. I mean, fair enough.

"Didn't you say something about biological adaptation?" I ask.

"Sorry Erica, but you're not the one who just grew a cock."

"But I am the one who was told she was a half orc yesterday," I throw back.

She nods, still panting. "I see your point. I see it, but I'm, um... having a moment."

I stand and step towards her. "I know this is probably pretty scary," I say. "But," I wrap a hand around her cock and pump gently, reaching up to kiss her pretty, plump lips. She's rock hard. She inhales sharply. "I don't think we should look a gift cock in the mouth."

I kneel and put her in my mouth. Her eyes close, and she puts a hand on my head, and makes a soft sound of air leaving her body. When I pull back, she's looking down at me. "I'm seeing the benefits of the situation." Her eyes are molten when she drags me to my feet and presses me against her. "Let's take it for a test drive."

She picks me up by my thighs, and I wrap my arms around her neck. She lays me down on the couch and kisses me gently, she spreads me and lines up between my thighs.

I hold my breath when she slowly breaches me. My eyes flutter shut, and I think I stop breathing when she finally reaches her hilt. I'm so wet, it doesn't hurt at all, but I feel extremely full. And somehow, fulfilled. The irritation that's been riding me all day has eased, like my body has been waiting for this.

"How is it?" she asks breathily.

"Heaven," I say, and my voice sounds drugged and hoarse. I don't think it can feel any better until she pumps in and out, her thumb lazily circling my clit. Then she speeds up, thrusting into me until we both cry out and release.

When she pulls out, fluid spills out of me. She stares at it. "I have no idea whether this can make you pregnant." My heart leaps at those words.

So far, with Olivia, I've let my body do the steering. But now my head, and my heart, clamor for attention. She's strong and sexy, and she would be a great mother. We both would. But she looks stunned.

I pull her down towards me. "Does that bother you?"

She meets my gaze and I find tears standing in her eyes. "No," she says, and kisses me fiercely.

THREE MONTHS LATER

ERICA

O livia's head is between my thighs, on our bed on the island. Cunnilingus won't get me pregnant, but she says she can't get enough of how I taste. I'm back at work, but we're on the island pretty frequently on the weekends these days. It's peaceful here, and other orcs are only slowly being moved here.

My eyes are closed, but I open them to look at the pregnancy test in my hand. "It's a yes," I say, and she lifts her head from between my legs.

"Really?" she asks, then shoots me a cheeky grin that makes my insides melt. "I beat my brother to it."

I roll my eyes at that. Their sibling rivalry is ridiculous. But then, I literally danced with joy when I was promoted above Cameron at work, so I understand petty competition.

But since I found out I'm a mystic, my priorities have shifted.

"Does this mean you'll move to the island full-time?" Olivia asks.

"I told you, I'm not built for a life of pampered leisure," I argue, not for the first time. Even if the number of zeroes in Olivia's bank account means I never have to work again.

"I know," Olivia says. "And I'm not expecting you to give up work entirely. But maybe shifting focus, like managing the island?"

I pause. The island is a big project, with a lot of moving parts. It would be challenging and look great on a resume. "I'm open to discussion," I say.

"Excellent!" Olivia grins at me like it's a done deal. She has absolutely no poker face. And with the next generation of orcs growing inside me, I have a feeling any negotiations I engage in for this new role are going to go my way.

That matters a whole lot less than it used to.

"How shall we celebrate?" she asks, climbing up my body. Her erection presses between my thighs, and I open my legs wider to let her in as we kiss.

"I'm sure you have some good ideas," I say, and throw my arms around her neck, letting the pregnancy test fall to the bed beside us.

KIDNAPPED BY THE ORC

L.A. MONTEIRO

CHAOS ELF PUBLISHING

Chapter One

EMILY

The first time I see an orc in real life is when one removes a black hood from my head. My hands are bound behind my back, but I'm otherwise unhurt. I gasp, my heart skittering in my chest.

He's big. Bigger than I thought he'd be. On the news, they look like large men. He's the largest person I've ever seen. And of course, green.

His small pointed tusks curl upwards along either jaw. They look sharp. His dark green hair is long and tied back at the nape of his neck. And he's wearing spectacles. That's unexpected. And he's handsome.

I dismiss my surprise. He's a kidnapper.

My eyes scan the room, desperate for details about where I am.

The room is plain and square, with no windows and only one closed door. Behind my captor is a single bed -

it's made up with deep red sheets and plush cushions. It looks sturdy, with a metal frame with slats at the head and a metal bar at the base. Metal cuffs are attached at each corner. My stomach drops at the sight of them.

My handbag is nowhere in sight.

Despite myself, my gaze is drawn back to him.

He steps back, and his expression is wary and curious rather than fierce. I take in his outfit of black slacks, shiny shoes and a white dress shirt open at the collar. The spectacles look too small on his face. He's dressed like he's about to step in to an office job.

Maybe he is? We could be anywhere. There's no sound of life beyond the walls of the room.

It smells clean in here, and it's cold. Or that might be because I've got low blood sugar. I was kidnapped on my way to a meal - not ideal for someone with diabetes.

The fear I've been trying to push down flutters in my stomach.

I knew I'd meet an orc eventually, since my sister, Summer, is one of the few mystics in existence, and engaged to the orc leader Tom Johnson. But I've been avoiding it for good reason. I'm probably a mystic too, and an orc is likely to trigger my heat. There's no way I'm ready for that.

Summer was worried orcs would attack me, but I assured her with extra locks, and Tom put more security in my apartment block and university.

None of that mattered.

He took me right off the street, in the middle of the day. I didn't see him then - a bag was thrown over my head and I was grabbed from behind and thrown over a shoulder.

Absurdly, my first thought was to worry I'd flash my thong, or my boobs would fall out of my light summer dress. But that was before I understood what was really happening. Or maybe it was my brain trying to protect me with normal thoughts instead of totally freaking out.

At least a dozen people must have seen him. That means people will be looking. I only have to hold tight until they find me. And hope for the best before then.

Tom told me his brother Evan is dangerous and has a missing arm. The one looking curiously at me right now has both his limbs.

"What do you want?" I ask, with more courage than I feel. A smart mouth, that's what my mother says I have. I tell her I'm smart in general, so why hide it?

"My name is Lachlan, Emily. I want to talk," he says. His voice is soft, his accent refined. If he weren't an orc, I would assume it was European. It takes me by surprise.

"Untying me might make for better conversation," I suggest.

"I would like you to stay while I talk," he says, with the ghost of a smile. It's a sad smile though, as if he regrets the situation.

Despite his green skin, his features are handsome, and he seems gentle. He moves like a human too, with unusual grace for his size.

"Why, so you can woo me into being your mystic queen? You haven't made the best first date impression," I say.

He raises both his hands in defense. "I see your point. But I wasn't sure if you'd come if I had asked. And I'm here on behalf of my king," he says. "He will be the one doing the wooing."

Of course, Tom's brother, who considers himself the rightful king, has sent someone to do his dirty work. I wonder if he sent someone he knew was attractive and well-spoken as a strategy to calm me. I wonder if the king himself is so polite.

"He couldn't send me flowers like a normal guy?"

He runs a hand over his hair and sighs. His muscles strain against... everything. He must have gotten the biggest sizes of everything. The guy is huge.

"I'm here to entreat you to assist our cause. We've been watching you."

"And that's not creepy at all."

He looks at me intensely. His eyes are light gold against his green skin. Their beauty startles me, and for a moment I can't look away.

Heat stirs in my core, shocking me into looking away. I haven't had much experience with men, but I've never had this reaction before. I was hoping to have more time before my body began reacting like a mystic.

Would I be like this with every orc? I try not to let my reaction show and hone in on the conversation again.

"Of course we're interested in you," he says passionately. "I wish to convince you to help our people, since you've shown no move to take up your rightful place as a mystic and breeder for my people."

"Breeder!" I bark a laugh. "You need to work on your pickup lines, buddy."

"You jest, but you're a student of biology, so I think you know it's true. You are the hope of my people." He says it softly, fervently.

My stomach flutters a little, and I curse my lady parts. I give him a hard stare. "So, what is this? You're trying to guilt me into a pity fuck?"

He winces. "No, I... I hoped you would grow to understand the cause of my people. If I reasoned with you..." he runs his hand over his hair again and pulls the black elastic in it free. He wraps it around his wrist and his hair flows freely around his shoulders.

I wouldn't have expected an orc to have such pretty hair. For a moment, I'm distracted by the way it falls around his neck, and the waft of scent as it flows free. It's a smoky tobacco scent, with an undercurrent of musk that makes my mouth water.

I breathe in deeply and blink myself back into reality. "Your king puts a lot of stock in reason if he thought you could talk me into breeding with him after being abducted."

"Yes, it is logical a kidnapping wouldn't win you over," he says dryly, as if irritated. Interesting.

"The reasoning was your idea," I say. It's not a question. His lips press together, which is confirmation enough.

"And anyway, I'm not yet ready to be a breeding machine for every hopeful and horny orc around."

He actually looks shocked. "It wouldn't be like that. You'd be revered. Wooed. My king was hopeful of making you his queen."

"Ah, then your plan was to chain me to one hopeful and horny orc."

"No, I..." he presses his lips together in exasperation. "You are understandably upset. You've been taken against your will and kept captive. I was here to introduce myself,

begin our conversation, and make you more comfortable."
He glances backwards at the bed.

My lady parts twinge in a reaction suspiciously like joy,
but my heart pounds in my chest. Lachlan doesn't seem
like a rapist, but if I'm going into heat, like I think I am,
it won't be long before I'm begging for his touch. My gaze
strays to his enormous hands. His claws have been neatly
trimmed and blunted, with big, thick fingers.

I don't know what expression I'm making, but he puts
his hand up as if soothing a scared animal.

"The bed isn't for..." he says. "We would like to talk to
you. I've been asked to teach you some of our history. But
you will need to sleep at some point, and we thought it best
if you were comfortable doing so."

"Sure, that's why you need the cuffs," I say. The
intensity of this whole situation is making my head swim,
and I'm not sure how long it's been since I ate. I feel faint,
my skin clammy with cold. This dress isn't covering nearly
enough of me.

He steps closer, looking concerned.

I kick him in the shin. It's pathetically weak.

He raises an eyebrow at me. "Really?"

Well, now I feel ridiculous. And with him this much
closer, I'm getting wafts of his spicy, masculine scent. It's
not helping my dizziness.

If I go into a diabetic coma, there's no way I'm getting out of here.

I shut my eyes. "If you want to talk, you'd better get me some insulin," I say. "Diabetic. There's a pen in my bag."

I assume he put it somewhere, but I can't see it. He frowns and goes to leave the room. "Hurry," I call to his retreating back.

Chapter Two

LACHLAN

Emily doesn't look good as I walk out the door, shutting it behind me. Humans aren't supposed to change color so quickly. I knew about her diabetes, but knowing and seeing are two different things.

Outside the room, I'm surrounded by a rough stone corridor, more like a cave than a building, but well lit by lines of fluorescents in the ceiling. There are three more white doors around me, while the cave extends into sunlight and a blue skyed forest at one end, and into a large dark cave at the other.

The room Emily's in and a few surrounding rooms were built within the past year, then abandoned.

They were designed to be used for school retreats, set into the caves. But the company building it discovered instability in the caves caused by deep tree roots and paused construction to investigate. They left behind a site with power and running water, but only a few rooms.

Evan is standing outside the door, pacing on the damp stone.

"What did you find out?" he growls. He's wearing a black dress shirt and pants. The cuff of his right arm hangs loose where his hand is missing. Across his left eye, a wicked scar makes him look fierce, especially above his square jaw, blunt nose and closely cropped hair.

He always dressed well in our world. We were more friends there, rather than king and servant. But he was a proud warrior then. He lost his hand and scarred his face shortly before we came to this world.

Without his hand, he couldn't shift into a human. So it was up to his brother Tom to pave our way in this world, and even when we came here, to represent the orcs amongst the humans. Tom, the clever second son.

When Evan arrived in this world with no hand, and saw what Tom had grown, Evan stepped aside for the good of all our people.

But as Tom accumulated more wealth, Evan slunk deeper into the background. He disagreed with Tom's business decisions - Evan thought some of Tom's wealth should be diverted into businesses that could employ our people. Evan also disagreed with Tom's strategy to separate the orcs from the humans. But when he tried to talk to Tom, he was met with dismissal and pushed aside.

In frustration, Evan built allies around himself, slowly gaining ground amongst the orcs to overthrow Tom's rule. But then Tom found a mystic, and support for Evan faded.

I serve the crown and the rightful king, but I've found myself hoping that Evan will see reason and stop his mad schemes to reclaim power. I still see the warrior in him - the king he used to be. And yet here we are.

"Humans don't like being tied up," I point out. He scowls at me, and I lower my eyes. He's still my leader, and my family has been loyal to his line for aeons. I might not approve of all his methods, but I obey. "We have talked very little. She's diabetic. She needs an insulin pen from her bag," I say.

"What the fuck does that mean?" he asks. The one thing he's adopted from the human world is the word fuck.

"It means she has a medical condition and I need to treat her, or she might get sick."

"There's something wrong with her, then?" He frowns. I can see the wheels turning. He's worried about her ability to breed.

Something in my chest twangs. She's scared and doesn't need his judgment. "There's nothing wrong with her," I say, walking ahead of him down the rough hallway to the cave we sleep in. I stashed Emily's bag there. He follows me. Our cots are pushed to either edge of the cave walls, and her bag is on my bed.

"She's perfectly healthy." I keep the irritation from my tone.

I fish around in the bag for her insulin pen. As an afterthought, I pick up the entire bag and put the pen back inside it. She'll feel safer having her things.

Evan's not happy about me speaking to her first, but he's had bad reactions from women in this world before, and he doesn't want to scare her off.

It's a compromise. He didn't listen to me about dropping this whole kidnapping idea. He's obsessed with getting a mystic pregnant before his brother does.

He follows me to the door of her cell, and I pause and look at him before I open it. I know what he's going to say. "I will come in with you."

"No, you won't. That wasn't the plan," I say. "For her to be your queen, she must be sympathetic to our cause. She must learn the ways of our people. And that means knowledge, not rutting."

"I didn't mean rutting," he growls low. "But if she is to be my queen, she should know me."

"She's terrified right now, and sick. Another orc in the room won't help. You know the reputation of our people - monsters. Let's not live up to it."

I yank the door open and shut it behind me, feeling only slightly conflicted. Do I genuinely think I can sell this woman on helping our people? Or am I just delaying the inevitable? The Evan I grew up with in our homeworld would not have forced himself on a woman or taken advantage of her heat. But this new Evan - I'm not so sure. And Emily is headstrong.

If she resists him, he may force things. Maybe I'm not yet ready to know how far Evan will go for power. Maybe I can prevent that from happening.

When I collect myself and turn to face her, her forehead is sweating. She's slumped against her bonds. Not for the first time, I feel a pang of guilt at seeing her arms bound behind her. People think we're savages, and right now we're living up to the reputation.

"Is this it?" I ask, holding the pen up out of her bag. I know it is - I've seen it online.

She nods, eyes closing shut gratefully, and takes a deep breath in relief.

I researched her and knew about her condition and am well versed in how to use these pens. I practiced on oranges. But she doesn't need to know how long we've been planning this abduction, or how much I've been watching her.

She's been hard not to admire from afar. She's focused, driven, intelligent and beautiful.

She's dark-haired and brown-skinned like her sister, but more slight and curvier. I've found myself enjoying the crinkle in her nose when she concentrates as much as the swell of her curves in the summer dresses she favors. Maybe that's why I've insisted on this time with her.

"I need my hands untied to stick myself," she says.

I hesitate only for a second, nod and stand behind the chair to untie her.

I could do it for her, but I want her to feel comfortable. Safe. She can't escape with me in the room, or with Evan outside.

Up close, her hair smells like a spicy fruit. It's strangely familiar. I resist the urge to sniff her, instead wondering at the softness of her brown skin as my fingers brush against hers. Goosebumps rise on her neck.

I push down the warm glow of satisfaction that rises in my belly when I realize she's reacting to me. She is not for me.

When her hands are free, I step back quickly.

She rubs her wrists and circles her shoulders, takes the pen, and jabs it into her arm. She doesn't even wince as the needle goes in, and she holds it there for a few moments.

"Is that better?" I ask.

She nods. The relief is palpable. I hand her the bag. She rifles through it.

"You've still got your phone, but the internet and phones won't work here," I say. She nods. I know phones are a comfort to the humans. I aim to comfort her where I can. "If you need anything, please ask me. We don't mean to hurt you, only to persuade you."

"And if you can't persuade me?" she asks, looking up at me through hooded eyes.

"I'm confident I will," I respond. It's a non-answer, but it's the only answer I have for her. I don't know what Evan will do if Emily doesn't come around. If she leaves we don't have another mystic, and that means Tom will almost certainly have a child before Evan, solidifying Tom's place on the throne.

But while we're still talking, she's safe.

Maybe that's why I'm not expecting it when she takes a lunge at me.

She's tiny. I'm more surprised than anything when she swipes at me with the small switchblade. She slices through my t-shirt and draws blood before I grab her wrist, bending her hand back on instinct until she drops the knife.

It's a simple thing to put a hand over her mouth before she can cry out in alarm, conscious of Evan nearby. If he thinks I can't handle her, he'll intervene before I'm ready.

She kicks and squirms in my grasp, but I yank on her twisted hand until she stills.

The scent of my blood is fresh in the air, and with her pressed so close, it mingles with the smell of her. It is flowers I know - flowers of my homeland - heady and sweet, but complex and multi-layered.

It makes me ache for home when I was still proud of the king I served. And when a young, ripe mystic like this one could offer me the tribute of her body, in an ancient ritual.

My sex swells instinctively.

But I'm not some youngling orc at the mercy of their senses. I know the difference between my physical desires and the logic of the moment. But Emily doesn't know me at all, and her surprising surge of violence means a lesson may be in order.

I press her against me, keeping a hand on her mouth, releasing her hand, and instead wrapping her tightly to me so she feels the physical arousal she's caused. I'm careful not to hurt her. "Did you know that fighting is an aspect of the orcish mating rituals?" I ask in her ear. She stops struggling and I smell the sharp pang of her fear, the way her body stiffens against me.

It's hard to keep going, but if Evan gets to her, it will be worse. He's been brutal with both male and female cadets in training before, and I don't know what he'll do with this human - how much he'll think she can handle.

"I won't hurt you, but you must understand the reaction that drawing blood brings," I say again, keeping my tone even. "I'm going to tie you to the bed now. If you struggle, I will put a hand over your nostrils until you pass out to make it easier. But I don't think that's necessary, do you?" She shakes her head against my hand.

I pull away from her. "Lie down on the bed, face up," I say. She does so, stiffly.

Guilt crawls at me. I push it down. This is for our people. Nothing is more important than that. I want to convince Emily to be on our side, but that can't happen if she keeps fighting me.

She lies down, and I fasten the manacles at her hands and feet. She can keep her legs closed and has a decent range of movement.

I step back as quickly as I can from her maddening scent.

"Now sit up," I say. She looks at me fearfully but does as I say. I pick the bag she discarded up from the floor and put it in her lap. I pick up the switchblade and close it, slipping it into my back pocket. "You'll be more comfortable there. There are blankets and pillows. I'll bring you food and water and escort you to the toilet three times a day. When your phone runs out of charge, I can charge it for you. I'll leave you some space, and I'll be back in a few minutes with something to eat."

I leave the room, locking the door behind me.

CHAPTER THREE

EMILY

It was stupid to lunge for Lachlan; I knew it even as I did it. But I've got no idea how many chances I'm going to get. He says he won't hurt me, and has provided me with insulin, but that's not the actual issue.

My body's reaction to him is scaring me.

When Summer first became a mystic her anxiety medication suppressed the change and made her lose control, but without the medication she would have gone into heat almost immediately.

I've thought long and hard about what I'd want if I were to turn. I want more control over it, not less. So, I researched animal heat and the medication Summer was on. And for the past three months, I've been researching how I can control my adrenaline.

Despite the insane situation I'm in, I close my eyes and focus on my breathing. My heart rate slows, and the spiraling thoughts in my head settle.

I feel human. Normal. No sign of any obvious changes. I lift my hands and open my eyes, inspecting them. They're still skin colored. I scan my body for any changes. Nothing. Except a thrill of what can only be called arousal in the pit of my stomach.

The press of Lachlan's body shocked me, but also thrilled me. His skin was hot - almost boiling. Thinking of him now, and his gentle but firm touch, makes my heartbeat pick up. I count my breaths, slowing them down.

In theory, I knew my body would react to orcs, but that wall of hard muscle, and his obvious arousal... it hit me hard.

I've never had much time for boyfriends. Summer was always looking for something - some meaning in her life. I wasn't like that. I knew where I was going and what I wanted.

I dated the odd guy in high school but we never went far. I thought maybe I'd find someone I was interested in at university, but none of the boys did it for me. Okay, if I'm entirely honest, I didn't think they were worth my time.

When Summer came out as a mystic, I wondered if the reason boys never interested me is that they were the wrong species.

My reaction to Lachlan is not good news. Summer said the heat could be painful if it isn't satisfied. She gets through hers with a loving partner. If my heat has been triggered, I'll be at the mercy of the orcs who've captured me. And whatever my body wants, I have no intention of rolling over and playing good little breeder.

Besides which, my attraction is to Lachlan, and I get the impression the orc I'm intended for isn't so gentle.

I'm happy I can shuffle in the bed, so I can pull my skirt down, suddenly self-conscious at the shortness of my dress. Lachlan will be back in a few minutes. The manacle chains clink together as I move.

I stand up, surprised they let me move that far.

The bed itself is surprisingly strong and bolted to the floor. There are no power points in the room - no sign of technology. I have no sign of where we are. When Lachlan opened the door, I was too worried about my insulin to notice what was beyond it.

I try the door handle. Locked, as expected. I press my eye to the keyhole and jump back as the handle moves.

Lachlan opens the door.

He's holding a tray with one hand with a ham sandwich and a glass of orange juice on it. He doesn't react to my position, just walks towards the bed and puts the tray down. "It's nothing special today - our chef is back tomorrow."

I look at him sharply, unsure if he's joking. His mouth curves into an uncertain smile, which fades quickly when I don't return it.

He stands back and watches me eat. I'm starving and I eat the food fast, the chains around my wrist clanking. When I look up at him again, I'm licking the last of the juice off my lips and catch him staring, his expression intent and predatory. I stop breathing.

My core twinges with need.

He inhales sharply and blinks, his gaze meeting mine and flitting away again. "Do you need the toilet? I can duck back in another hour if you don't need to go now."

"I'll go now," I say, swallowing hard. I need some fresh air. And I want to see what's outside these four walls.

⚜

When Lachlan opens the door, I'm confused by the cave-like floor outside the room. And then I realize there's sunlight... partly blocked by another hulking orc.

He's lounging against the wall opposite us. His gaze is hard, and he's got a missing hand. He smiles, and it comes out like a leer. His nostrils flare. "I thought it was time we met, Emily. I'm Evan," he says. It sounds like a threat.

I hold my breath and meet his red gaze. I'm known for my sassy mouth, but right now I have nothing to say. This is the orc who ordered me kidnapped, and there's no sense of compromise in the lines of his body.

A pressure starts in my chest, and it's hard to breathe. Yes, I'm angry, but it's overridden by fear. Something about this orc makes me want to run in the opposite direction.

My gaze leaves him, looking for safety, and I spot the clearly marked bathroom door in the room next to the one I just left. I turn away from him, towards it for safety, and he grabs my arm. His fingers dig into me, and I turn to face him, hoping terror isn't written in my eyes.

"Aren't you going to say hello?" he asks. His eyes are flinty, resentful. He won't let me go until he gets what he wants. I can feel it as much as if he said it out loud.

"Let her go, Evan," Lachlan says behind him, and yanks Evan's arm away. I flee into the bathroom.

Inside, I press myself back against the door. It's clean and white inside, and blissfully empty. I slide to the floor. My hands are shaking.

I won't survive in this state for long - despite just having insulin, I feel like my blood sugar is diving. I don't know how diabetes interacts with orcish heat.

If I'm passed out, Evan can do whatever he wants to me. My shaking body feels cold at the thought. I have no idea how much time I have left.

Still feeling shaky, I use the toilet and slow my breaths.

I need to run. Now. Evan won't care about my compliance. He won't be gentle, or considerate, if I go into heat.

Every time I'm untied is a chance to run.

I finish in the toilet, run the tap and press my ear to the door outside. It's quiet.

This is my chance.

I rip the door open and turn to the outside entrance. Lachlan and Evan are standing there, whispering fiercely to each other. They don't see me yet, but there's no way I can get past them.

I'm caught. Maybe I should give up now. I can't get past them to freedom, and behind me is only a cave. Then Evan growls, low in his throat, and panic grips me.

I turn, and run, into the darkness beyond this small strip of hallway - into the cave.

Chapter Four

LACHLAN

"Fuck," Evan says, as I run after her.

"Stay here," I yell at him. "The caves aren't stable."

He ignores me - of course he does, so I run ahead of him, after Emily. The cave floor is dry and even, and I follow the sound of her panting breath, the flash of her white dress, and the scent of her, until the cave slants down.

It's colder here, and the walls close in from an enormous cavern into a small pathway. She's slowed down, but she's still some way ahead of me when the caves branch off in two directions.

One has a smaller entrance. It will be a squeeze for me to go in there, but it's clear that's the route Emily took. I explored these caves before we moved in - there isn't much beyond there but a cave with a natural pool, about the size of a room.

I look through the cave entrance. It's astonishing she can see at all, in the dark. My orc senses are giving me dim night vision. She's walking her hands along the walls of the cave, looking for an exit that isn't there.

"Emily," I call out. "These caves are unstable, and there's no way out. Please come back."

Behind me, I can hear Evan following me. He isn't making much noise. We don't know how much instability there is.

She doesn't respond. I could wait her out. But even in the darkness, I see her find a crack in the smaller cave. I've been unable to get in to explore. If she gets further into the caves, we may not be able to get her out. What if she passes out with her diabetes? She'll be stuck.

The thought drives me on.

I hold my breath and squeeze through the cave entrance, scraping my shoulders and head. When I break my way in, she's still there - the exit she found is too narrow for her to fit through.

"Come back to the room," I say gently.

She's pressed back against the cave wall, but I have her attention. "We won't hurt you."

Behind me, Evan reaches the entrance to the cave and calls out, "Do you have her?" Her gaze flits to the sound of his voice, eyes wide and nostrils flared in alarm.

My expression hardens and I'm glad neither of them can see it. "She's coming out now," I say, and step towards Emily slowly. Her head swings towards me. She can't see much, but she can hear the crunch of sand and small stones under my feet.

There's a grunting behind me as Evan tries to force his way into the cave. Her face shifts to his rough grunting noises in the darkness and she sinks to the ground, holding her knees. My heart goes out to her, and I call to him. "No need to come in, Evan. I will bring her out."

He curses and smacks a fist against the rock in front of him.

A low rumbling sound echoes from his fist to the chamber around us and we all freeze.

When the rock slides around us, I lunge towards Emily and wrap my arms around her while Evan shouts.

By the time the dust clears, Emily and I are left with little space, and Evan is nowhere to be seen. The entrance is gone.

CHAPTER FIVE

EMILY

Lachlan's arms wrap around me while the cave collapses. I shiver against him, fear like a white heat in my spine, breathing in the dizzying scent of him and willing the world away.

When the cave stops rumbling, Lachlan whispers in my ear. "Are you okay?"

I take a moment to find my voice, and I clear my throat when I do. "Relatively speaking," I whisper back. I'm not quite ready when his hard body unwraps from me and I have to face reality.

The cave is pitch dark, but Lachlan's thumb rubs against my cheek as if he can see me. "I'm sorry, Emily. I should have told you these caves are unsafe." His hand is gentle and my emotions tumble in confusion at his apology. He is my kidnapper, and this small apology shouldn't move me.

A moment later I'm blinking into the light. He's turned his phone torch on. "The battery won't last forever, but we can see if there's a way out."

We're both covered in dust. The cave mouth has collapsed, and we're left with about half a small room, with enough room to stand and stretch our legs. There is no opening - this much is clear while Lachlan walks around the cave, shining a light into every crack and crevice. "Nothing," he says.

I stand and brush dust out of my hair. Almost immediately I feel faint, and reach a hand out to steady myself.

Lachlan's with me in a second, hands on my cheeks, concerned eyes roaming my face. "What is it?" I must be pale because he says, "You just had insulin."

I lean into him and let him lead me to sit down again on the cave floor. "Don't know how it works with my..." I slur but can't finish the sentence. I can't tell him I'm in heat. I'm barely ready to face it myself.

Better just to leave it unsaid for now. He feels warm and nice, and I feel safe with him. And he smells divine. Besides, what can we do now? We're trapped in a cave. My eyes slip closed.

He slaps my face. "Emily, stay awake," he orders. I frown resentfully at him, but I feel more awake. His golden eyes are crinkled at the edges with worry for me.

"First you kidnap me, and now you won't let me rest," I say, hand to my cheek. I'm aware I sound like a cranky child, but I don't care. I'm exhausted and scared and I deserve to complain. "And you were going to deliver me to that... that monster." The thought of Evan sobers me further.

"I'm sorry," he says. A muscle in his jaw clenches as he looks around the cave. Anywhere but at me. "My family has served Evan's since I was a child. He is my liege. And at some point, he meant the best for his people..." He shakes his head. "He's not the same orc I used to know. He grew bitter, watching his brother shine in this world. I should not have agreed to him taking you."

His mouth is turned down in unhappiness, his eyes downcast as he makes his confession. It feels genuine. Or maybe I just want it to be - we are trapped here, after all, and I could get used to the feel of him wrapped around me. But how can I forgive a kidnapping so quickly?

"I would make an excellent queen," I say instead.

He catches my gaze then and gives me a grateful half grin that makes me tingle all over, but particularly between my legs. I have to work to control my breathing, slowing down my skittering heartbeat.

I officially have a crush on my orc kidnapper. How embarrassing.

I look around the cave again and take a breath. I'm feeling much more awake than I was a few minutes ago, but it doesn't change our situation.

We're stuck here, with no way out, for only knows how long.

I've always been the smart one in my family - the one with all the answers. But there isn't an answer out of this.

I'm about to go into heat. And I have no idea how my diabetes will interact with my orcish nature. I've had no control since Lachlan dragged me off the street.

I should hate him, but my body doesn't care. All my control means nothing in this moment. The sensation between my legs is more like a burning now, and a cramp is starting deep in my belly.

I can barely think straight, which is weird for me. But amongst my fragmented thoughts, I can't help but wonder - what will it be like to give in to it?

By the time my gaze strays back to his, my body is on fire, and the worried crinkle in his forehead is the sexiest thing I've ever seen. My brain shuts off as I lean forward and kiss him.

Chapter Six

LACHLAN

Emily leans forward and presses her lips to mine. It's hesitant at first, her soft lips tenuous. In that kiss, I feel her uncertainty. I stay still, letting her decide.

She is braver than I have ever been, in this moment, and it humbles and shames me.

This is why I watched her so greedily, so fascinated at her freedom and joy out in the human world. Emily is a woman living a life she chooses, as I have always yearned to live.

Even in this moment, with few choices available, she's taking action - conscious, careful action. As I have failed to act for the past four years, serving Evan.

But I took her for me, not for him. I realize that now, in a rush of guilt.

I receive her gift gratefully, ignoring the fire that rages in my blood and the crashing revelations she has opened into my soul.

When she opens her mouth, I gratefully allow her to explore my lips, my mouth, my tongue, while I drown in her complex floral scent.

My cock is painfully hard in my pants, and I long to press her to the cave floor and taste her everywhere. To own her, and have her own me, so that I can pledge my loyalty to the only person I wish to serve again.

But instead, my muscles tense with control as I let her ease closer, pressing her small body against mine. Only then do I let my hands slip to her back, blissfully exploring her soft skin.

The scrapes from the rocks have left a sting to my skin and the tang of blood in the air, intensifying every second between us.

The only sound in the cave is our breathing.

She deepens her kiss, sucking and nipping on my lower lip, and by now I'm sure she can feel my rock-hard erection pressed between us as I let my hands travel lower, gripping her round buttocks and sliding along her exposed thigh.

Her nipples are hard against my chest when I feel her nails dig into my back. My groan is loud in the still air, and she pulls back.

Even in the dim light, I can see her skin is green, her limbs elongated, her muscle thicker and finer. And she's grinning at me with mischievous red eyes.

"I thought that might work," she says, and scrambles to stand up and stare at her own hands, her limbs, and around her at the cave.

I'm left dazed, my world shattered, my heart pounding, trying to pull myself together.

"My vision is so much better like this," she wonders. Her eyes don't look at me again. "And it took care of my diabetes. Handy trick."

I swallow but find myself unable to speak.

I want to beg her to come back to take care of my straining cock, and so I can take care of the wetness I can smell between her legs. But she is the master here, and I am the servant. I have already trapped her once against her will, and I don't intend to do it again. So, I merely lick my lips and track her with my eyes, waiting until she's ready for me again.

She's not acting like a mystic in heat, despite the change - I've heard they lose all reason, and desperately need release. She's acting like a scientist, exploring her new senses. But I can see the signs - the shake of her hand, the sweat beading on her forehead, her dilated pupils. Not to mention the transformation into an orc. She is in heat - but she's holding it in. And it's costing her. That thought spurs me to act.

She reaches out to touch the rock, facing away from me. I stand and go to her, putting a hand on her shoulder gently, so gently. "Emily," I say. She turns to me, and I tip her chin until she's meeting my gaze. I want to tell her nothing will happen without her say so, that I'm sorry again, that I took her choices away from her, that I've wanted to touch her skin since the first moment I saw her.

But instead, an orc fist bursts through the cave wall with a crashing sound.

She gasps and jumps back, away from both the fist and me.

"Lachlan!" The fist disappears and Evan's face appears. There's a decent sized hole in the rock now - big enough for Emily to crawl through, but neither Evan nor me.

His eyes light up when he sees Emily's new form. Her dress is shorter on her new body. I stand in front of her, blocking his gaze from her bare green skin.

He doesn't seem to notice. He laughs.

My skin prickles with the urge to commit violence. I want to rip the eyes from his head. But he stands between us and freedom. "Can you get out, Evan?" I ask, voice tight.

He shakes his head. "I don't know yet. I couldn't figure out which way I was punching. But I'm glad I went this way, first." His eyes sear into Emily, past me. "Heat or no, you can take my cock in that form."

I snarl. It's the first time I've ever snarled at Evan. He looks at me in surprise. "It looks like someone's in heat. So, I won't hold that against you, Lachlan. If you pass her through to me now."

Emily's eyes flick between the two of us, backing away, eyes fearful.

My stomach sinks when I realise she thinks I will give her to him.

But then why wouldn't she believe it? I dragged her here to serve him. She doesn't know how quickly she's overridden my loyalties with one sweet, lingering kiss.

But actions speak louder than words.

I step forward and punch Evan in the nose, through the hole in the wall. "You will not touch her while I'm alive."

He roars, and the cave shudders. We all look up, expecting another cave in, but the rumbles keep coming, and light creeps in from behind Evan. The wall behind him is open again - he's free. He looks behind him, and then back at me. The surrounding walls are still moving.

His nose is bleeding. He casts a scathing glance at Emily before his gaze returns to me. "Hope she's worth it," he says, then turns and runs away.

A few moments later, the cave shudders again, and I throw myself around Emily as dust and rocks falls from the ceiling.

CHAPTER SEVEN

EMILY

When the earth stops moving, Lachlan is on top of me and there's almost no room to move. I should feel claustrophobic, but my orc senses mean I can see, and my mystic heat means my survival instinct is zeroed in on only one thing.

It was all too new before, too fast, when I roamed the room with my new senses before. This thing rising in me... it's so raw. I wanted to rip my nails into his flesh and taste his blood.

I wanted to make my own decision about going into heat. I was going to wait until I was ready. Now I know, I was never going to be ready for this.

Lachlan's erection presses into my thigh. "Are you okay?" he asks. He lifts his weight off me, giving me space to breathe. His glasses are askew, his hair loose and flowing around his neck. And his golden eyes are looking at me like I'm the most important thing in the world.

I kiss him in response. The tight proximity means his scent is everywhere. The metallic tang of his blood from where the falling rocks cut him, mixing with his smoky tobacco scent. I'm drowning in him as I rip his shirt open, running my hands over his chest and around to claw at his back. Fresh wetness floods my drenched g-string.

He snarls as my claws draw blood. But he pulls back, pauses, and straightens his glasses. "Do you... want this?" he asks.

I appreciate the breathing room. This isn't how I thought my first time would be. But then what did I think it would be like? Awkward and sweet, with an undergraduate fumbling with my bra clasp? Instead, I'm pressed against an orc I barely know while we wait out our last breaths. It's hard not to let my hands trail along his chest, as I think.

"What did you think of me when you watched me?" I blurt out.

He blinks, and he purses his lips, considering. He pulls his body back further, and I resist the urge to claw him again, to pull him closer. "You are a vibrant woman with life still ahead of you. You were safe, flourishing. Capable of greatness. And bold. Bolder than me. I admired you. I still admire you." His gaze is fixed on mine, and I find it impossible to look away. His expression is grave, intense. Then the corner of his mouth kicks up. "And you could probably use a few more pens." I cough a laugh. I'm always losing pens.

"And now?" I ask. I hold my breath. Nothing should matter when we're in this position. But it does. It matters so much.

"That you are mine," he says, with a ferocity edged with steel. "And I would die for you," he says.

His fierce words unleash me, and I kiss him again. But it's his turn to claim me, and I groan when he presses me to the floor with a hand at my throat. Fresh wetness floods my sodden g-string.

He releases my throat to rip my dress apart, spilling my breasts into the icy darkness. My head falls back and my eyes flutter closed as he bends down to suck and lap at my tight nipples.

I'm whimpering by the time he kisses his way to my sex. He makes quick work of my g-string, and I can't help but think of his strong, thick fingers as the delicate fabric tears.

Then he spreads me open and devours my sex. My fingers twine through his long hair, and he grunts in pain even as he feasts on me.

My body shudders with pleasure, but it's not enough. A building ache in my core cries out in a demand I know only he can satisfy, and I writhe underneath him restlessly and hiss in frustration.

When his hand is back on my throat, I fall still. "I know what you want, my mystic," he says, as his thick fingers breach me for the first time. I arch up and cry out, nails digging into any part of his flesh I can reach to mark him as mine.

It hurts, and when the tang of my blood hits the air, his eyes widen in realization. "It is your first time."

"Yes," I say.

"Then we will take our time," he says, and releases my throat again. His fingers still inside me, he shuffles so his tongue gently works my clitoris.

My body easily accommodates him as my pleasure rises, and his fingers work me open, his tongue still lapping at me. When he reaches three fingers, the coil of rising pleasure within me is so tight it's almost painful. I beg, but he ignores me and works me slowly, gently.

The air is still around us, and there's no movement anywhere outside in the cave. We fill the small space, and it's as if the entire world is only us.

"Please Lachlan, please fuck me," I beg again.

"Almost, my mystic," he says, and presses another finger inside me. My eyes roll back, my back arches, and my sex is drenched. Even so, release does not find me.

When he takes his pants off, I'm more than ready. His cock is huge, and my mouth waters when it springs free from his underwear. I want to feast on him, lick along his thick length and claim him in that way, and I know that at some point I will. But right now, my own pleasure needs sating, and I need release more desperately than I need to claim him.

With me still on my back, he lines himself up and enters me slowly, oh so slowly. I hold my breath, and he whispers to me to breathe.

I remember my meditation, and close my eyes, breathing slowly and deeply, feeling every inch of him entering me. It feels deliciously full, but thanks to his patience, it doesn't hurt.

Then he moves out for the first time. My eyes spring open and I meet his molten gaze, intent on my face. "Now, you are ready," he says, and drives into me again.

I cry out and hold on to his shoulders as my core tightens in pleasure. This is what I've been waiting for - my body sings as he takes me. Soon I'm crying his name in a litany of pleasure, heedless of the risk of a cave-in around us.

Still Lachlan doesn't relent. As patient as he was before, he is now relentless, unleashing himself into me, and driving my ecstasy to new highs.

My core spasms fiercely and clenches around him as ecstasy washes over me. I clutch at him, holding on as if I might be swept away, and he kisses me as I quiver in the aftermath.

When we're spent, he cradles me close, until we both fall asleep.

***

We are woken by the earth moving around us again. I cry out in fear, and Lachlan grabs my face, kissing me and holding my gaze. "I will die happy in your arms," he says, and in our last moments, as the rubble rains down around us.

I whisper, "I love you." I've meant nothing more.

Vines reach down through the rocks and rip them away until sunlight is leaking in to us from above. I clutch to Lachlan as the vines wrap around us and lift us free into the light.

THREE MONTHS LATER

EMILY

"Are you sure about this?" Summer fusses with my collar, and I smack her hand away.

"Yes," I say firmly. We're on the roof on one of Tom's buildings, in a small room next to the very loud, very windy helicopter getting ready outside. Lachlan puts his hands on my shoulders. I look back at him and smile.

"Lachlan will be with me the whole time," I assure her.

"My genius sister," she says, and her lip quivers before she hugs me.

She's been like this since they pulled us out of the cave. Well, her friend Cassia pulled us out of the cave with her were-vine powers. Apparently, magic is real and so are were-vines. Add that to the list of weird and wonderful things I'm discovering now I'm a mystic.

"Okay, I guess this is it then," she says, and wipes a tear away. "Take care of her," she says to Lachlan.

"I will," he says gravely, and takes my hand. We open the door to a flood of sound and wind as we make our way to the helicopter.

I can understand why Summer's concerned. I'm the logical one - the reasonable one. Not the one you expect to rush things. But since Lachlan and I met, I'm understanding there are benefits to letting my heart and body take the reins.

And our people - the orcs - are suffering.

I look over at Lachlan when we strap into the helicopter seats. He smiles at me with a twinkle in his eye and I can't help grinning back like a lovesick, sex-addled fool. We're both excited.

My heat is almost upon me again. And I'm heading to the new facility Tom is building for the orcs - on an island, totally secluded. To get myself fully checked out, and get my human birth control removed, so we can start a family.

Since I found out Summer was orcish, I've known I wanted to help the orcs. I just wasn't expecting to find love, too.

More by the Author

The Zodiac Monster Romance Series

Taken by Aries

Taken by Taurus

Taken by Gemini

The Seasonal Spice Series

Taming the Office Orc (Prequel)

50 Shades of Orc

Bound by the Mages

The Witch's Tangle

Mated to the Sapphic Orc

Kidnapped by the Orc

Claimed by the Orc

Springvale Book Club

Hot for the Bad Boys

Hot for the Mafia Men

Standalones

The Wild Side

Anthologies

Lights

Batteries

Silk

www.ingramcontent.com/pod-product-compliance
Lightning Source LLC
Chambersburg PA
CBHW070322120726
47909CB00008B/2560